CARA COOPER

THE GHOST IN THE WINDOW

Complete and Unabridged

LINFORD
Leicester

First published in Great Britain in 2020

First Linford Edition
published 2021

A catalogue record for this book is available
from the British Library.

ISBN 978–1–4448–4636–2

Published by
Ulverscroft Limited
Anstey, Leicestershire

Set by Words & Graphics Ltd.
Anstey, Leicestershire
Printed and bound in Great Britain by
TJ Books Ltd., Padstow, Cornwall

This book is printed on acid-free paper

A Challenge Ahead

'What you need is a holiday.'

'What I need is to work. It's always work which helps me get over any . . . ' Siobhan Frost had nearly said, 'disasters', but didn't want to start another conversation about the Big, Bad Thing.

Her mother glanced at her but didn't probe. Having a career girl for a daughter, one who never seemed ready to settle down, worried her but Caroline knew better than to ask Siobhan too many questions.

That only made Siobhan clam up more about her private life.

Caroline had driven Siobhan to the airport and now they stood studying the departure board. October travellers scurried around them like ants over biscuit crumbs. The flight to Bordeaux, in the south west of France, left in 45 minutes. Just that name conjured up thoughts of sun and laughter for Siobhan which was exactly what she needed.

'Thanks for helping me, Mum, I've got a good feeling about this job. I can't believe how lucky I was to be chosen as the continuity person for 'Hallowe'en Hideaway'.

'Roger Rivers is a fantastic film director, one of the best in the business. And the setting looks fabulous in the photos he sent me. I'm itching to get there.'

'I'm sure you'll do a terrific job, darling, and an old manor house by a river in deepest rural France sounds idyllic. It's just that I was hoping by now to have a son-in-law, and to see you settled, not gallivanting off round the world again.' Caroline Frost sighed as she gave Siobhan one of those doleful looks she did so well.

At times Siobhan wondered who was the parent and who was the child. Her mother had never really grown up. Even now Caroline's hennaed hair was tied up in a green and yellow scarf with a wonky bow at the top and her chunky cerise fun fur coat was right out of the 1970s.

Siobhan's own style was a version of her mother's but done with much more restraint so that she looked arty but elegant. Moss green moleskin trousers, roomy but nipped in at the waist were topped with a loose heavy cream silk shirt. Highly polished Spanish leather brogues were laced at her feet above black socks with bows at the ankle. The whole was topped with the softest of tan suede jackets.

Siobhan's own hair was tamed with an elegant silk paisley scarf in woodland colours, knotted at the nape of the neck to drift down her back. She looked as if she had just emerged from an art and design school in 1930s Paris.

Siobhan bit her lip. She was going away so she wanted the mother and daughter farewells to be good. Her poor mother always seemed to be waving her off to somewhere in the world. A tiff at the last moment would make the parting so much more painful.

Siobhan knew the cancelled wedding had upset her mother more than Caroline dared say. At twenty-nine, Siobhan felt the pressure to be producing a grandchild for Caroline to fuss over but Siobhan wondered now after the break-up with Gerrard if that would ever happen.

Siobhan had always been independent, the head girl at school, then leaving home at eighteen to earn her own living as a runner for a TV studio. But film was her passion. She had climbed up from one job to another and now was in an enviable role co-ordinating continuity on the big films.

She made sure the props for scenes remained the same from one shot to the next and that they had not moved so that the action appeared to move seamlessly.

Famous actors had become part of her daily life and she'd been lucky enough to work in some dream settings, everything from parched deserts to snowy mountains. Each job was a new adventure, and she was itching to get away on this one. There was nothing like a new film to banish thoughts of a failed love affair.

'There's the check-in desk for my flight, Mum. I'll be fine now, really I will.'

Caroline touched her daughter's cheek.

'Are you sure this is the right thing to do, Siobhan? Couldn't you and Gerrard have just talked things through one more time?'

Siobhan grasped her mum's hand, squeezed it and placed a kiss, noting the bright purple nail varnish with a smile.

'Mum, please just accept that settling down with Gerrard had seemed attractive and so had he, but in reality it would have never worked out. He wouldn't have made me happy and I certainly wouldn't have made him happy. In fact, we'd have probably ended up murdering each other.'

Siobhan wheeled the small green case she'd bought in New York over to the check-in desk and handed over her passport.

'We did talk about things, Mum, endlessly. The fact is you can't make a rotten relationship into a fabulous one just by talking.' She squeezed her mother tight.

'Please give me some credit for being brave enough to pull out. France isn't far and I'll only be there for a couple of months. You can come and visit if you want. I'll be the first of the film people in the house. It's going to be a real challenge.

'La Refuge has been shut up for years like a hidden treasure and it's full of its original contents from centuries back. One of the things I have to do is get there first and suss out all the props. I have a list as long as your arm. I'll be so busy I don't even think I'll worry that the place is meant to be haunted.'

'Haunted?' Caroline shrieked. 'You

didn't tell me that.'

Siobhan wished she'd bitten the words back as soon as she'd opened her mouth. Caroline was the sort of mother who'd called an ambulance for her daughter when she'd only fallen off the bed. A born worrier, now she had something else to worry about.

'It's a silly rumour. It's all tosh, Mum — though it won't do the publicity for the film any harm. A film about Hallowe'en should have a haunting, shouldn't it?'

The ground crew stewardess tagged Siobhan's case, gave her a radiant smile and pointed her to the departure lounge. As they walked to the security check-in, Siobhan noted Caroline slowing down, like a child, delaying the moment a fraction longer.

'Why do you always push yourself, darling? They seem to be asking a lot of you, these film people. Staying in a great big haunted house all on your own? Why can't you get yourself an easier job?'

'Oh, I shan't be entirely on my own. There's some Frenchman who looks after the house and I'll be getting someone in to clean and get it ready. I'm sure they'll make me welcome.'

As Siobhan waved goodbye, she felt her heart contract. Her mother was making such efforts to look happy at her going while wiping away tears with a spotted handkerchief. She had always been encouraging.

They both knew why Siobhan drove herself so hard. Her father had predicted great things for his daughter. Just because a cruel unexpected stroke had cut short his life, didn't mean to say that Siobhan shouldn't meet his high expectations.

'You'll go places, Siobhan, you'll do exciting things, we'll never see the grass grow under your feet. Do all the things I wanted to do. Live life to the full.' His smile came back to her now as she breathed deeply, forgot Gerrard and strode ahead towards gate number 10.

A Face at the Window

Siobhan sat back in her seat and felt a tinge of regret that air travel was no longer a luxury pursuit. The grey and garish orange of the budget airline jarred. Everyone was plugged into their iPods instead of talking to each other and it made her pleased the flight would be shorter than the transatlantic ones she had been on to America.

Nevertheless, the two air stewards were kind to her and chatted about the places they had seen.

'You say you're staying in the country-side. Where's your nearest town?'

'Thiviers,' she replied, studying again the letter she had been sent with the details. 'I'm three miles outside.'

'How gorgeous,' the steward said, leaning on the headrest and chatting, 'with some serious countryside. Thiviers is surrounded by proper forests, with deer and wild boar.

'They make the most mouth-watering sausages. You must be sure to go towards Limoges as well where you can see beautiful porcelain tea-sets being made. I bought a superb one for my aunt, and she was bowled over.'

As he wittered on, hands fluttering like birds in the air, Siobhan thought of the letter the producer had sent her. She had read it at least five times. It had become like a talisman of good luck, something to hang on to when teary eyed she had been cancelling the church and writing to tell everyone her wedding was off.

The letter had been a ray of hope, promising that life still went on even after her private life was in tatters.

'You will be required to open up the house and arrange the cleaning and polishing of the props, all of which are already in the house,' the letter had stated.

'La Refuge is perfect for our needs. It was built centuries ago by the owner of a porcelain works. The old works with its tall chimney can be seen from the house and the two are connected by a river running through the grounds.

'The place has been empty for over 50 years apart from a short stay by the present owner, who moved out saying it was haunted. He has pots of money and had started to make changes, building a pool and pool house in the grounds before deciding the place was too isolated.

'He is much happier in his Paris home and will be selling La Refuge after we've filmed there. He didn't even stay long enough to sell any of the items, which are just as they were when the house was closed.

'Because the house has been shut up, all the upholstery, paintings and furniture have been beautifully preserved apart from having been buried under decades of dust.

'A French overseer called Christian Lavelle has looked after the house for the last 10 years making sure it stays secure and watertight. He lives in a small farmhouse within the grounds. He has the keys and will be on hand to look after you.'

* * *

At Bordeaux airport, Siobhan picked up a hire car and navigated her way on to the autoroute. It was a struggle remembering to stay on the right side of the road. Thank heaven for the satnav, she thought.

Sometimes her own independence made Siobhan peeved at herself for not accepting more help. Being a career girl was all very well but it kept her on edge most of the time. Still, as she settled on to the excellent French roads and switched on the radio she began to feel more relaxed.

Two hours passed before she reached Thiviers. As she turned off the motorway, she had a rude awakening. Suddenly the old world met the new as there was a steep climb up cobbled back roads where two cars could only narrowly pass. Hair-raising was not the word.

When she emerged from the cramped medieval road into the town square with its big old church and neatly clipped plane trees she was pleased La Refuge was only 15 minutes' drive away. What a change there was in those 15 minutes.

Siobhan passed farmhouses with cows, and pasture so green in the blazing sun it hurt her eyes. Then came thickening forest and finally she turned on to a road dark with low branched beech, and pine trees higher than telegraph poles.

Finally a carved sign proudly announced *La Refuge* and she turned right to see tall iron gates hanging from imposing stone pillars.

As she got out to open the gates and stretch her stiffened limbs, she suddenly felt the isolation of the setting keenly. How different this was from the city she was used to, and even from the bustling town she had just been through.

There was not a soul in sight, not a barking dog to be heard, just a bird which swooped from one sighing branch to the other.

Getting back into the car, Siobhan edged it down the pebble drive but stopped and parked once she was through the gates. The setting was so calm with barely a breeze, it seemed a violation to drive the noisy car right to the house and she decided instead to walk. She needed the exercise. Her cases could wait.

Pacing down the slope, she skirted around towering trees, picking her way carefully, eyes on the ground. She was more used to city pavements than this uneven country terrain. Then, as the view unfolded in front of her where the trees parted, La Refuge opened up in all its glory.

The house was more than imposing. Covered in creeping vines, and three storeys high, it had an enormous balustraded flight of steps to the entrance. Whoever built the place had set out to proclaim their wealth. The house was raised on a grassy mound as if standing on a pedestal. Surrounding it were majestic trees standing like sentinels on guard.

The whole edifice was a fitting testament to the faded grandeur of the owner who had built it. There was power in that house, and endless stories of the lives lived there, of births, deaths and marriages, of the miseries and the joys of simply being human.

The dramas of people never changed, Siobhan thought. There were endings and beginnings and this was a new beginning for her.

In the distance Siobhan heard the rush of a weir, and as she walked around the side of the house. There was a sweep of stretching lawns, bordered by a river. It reminded her of a blue satin ribbon as it undulated around the lawns and down to the warm red bricks of the porcelain works.

This river would have provided all

the water for a large household and a thriving little porcelain manufacturing building.

A footbridge led to the house. It spanned a stream from the hills which was only a trickle now it was high summer edging into autumn. Canoes sat by a boathouse. The setting took her breath away, so beautiful, so hidden.

'Mademoiselle.'

Siobhan almost jumped out of her skin and turned. She couldn't have been more surprised if the ghost of the original owner had stepped out of its white stone walls, in riding boots and long-tailed coat, hand outstretched to meet her.

Instead, a young man around her own age stood before her as solid and real as the sturdy oak trees.

'Christian Lavelle,' the man announced with a curt nod. He wore blue jeans, a blue denim shirt and smelled deliciously of fresh squeezed lemons and cedar-wood aftershave. His lustrous hair was swept back just touching his collar and curling at the edges. Long black lashes fringed his eyes.

'You frightened me,' Siobhan declared.

'I did not mean to.' His Gallic accent played underneath practiced English as he shook her hand. 'You must be Miss Frost. I am pleased to meet you. I see the house already has you under its spell.'

'I was miles away. It's so quiet here, apart from the river rushing by.'

'The two of them are like brother and sister, the house and the river — one wouldn't be here without the other.'

'How so?'

He leaned heavily on one leg, hand resting at his wide leather belt, relaxed in his own skin.

'It was the taming of the river which allowed the owner of the porcelain works to marshal the power of the water for his own use. Come, permit me to show you.'

Siobhan followed him round the extensive grounds, across the expanse of lawn and down to the riverbank hugging the garden. His gait was easy, relaxed as a horse making its way lazily to drink in a still pond.

Siobhan found herself looking a little longer than was polite at the slender hips and strong wide back. She forced her focus away, concentrating instead on the willow dipping into the water like fingers dangled over the side of a boat.

Her reaction to Christian surprised her. She certainly wasn't over Gerrard but her ex's slightly paunchy frame, over-indulged with too much champagne and smoked salmon, wasn't half as attractive as Christian's leanness. Though still a handsome man, her ex-fiancé Gerrard had succumbed too often to lavish business lunches.

The man striding before her now had a body to make any woman look twice. No, make that three times. It was honed and taut. She suspected that if Christian Lavelle drank wine, it would be a gutsy red, imbibed in great gulps after a day's hard work chopping trees and hauling logs.

'You see how calm and slow the river is here at the bottom of the garden. It flows faster past the building with the chimney.'

They'd walked behind a tall bank of trees to look at the huddle of red brick buildings at the edge of the estate.

'That's where the porcelain was mixed and fired. The porcelain works are all quiet and locked up now but at one time these outhouses would have been the thriving living quarters of workers from the factory. There was even a mill here to grind the flour for bread to feed them. The works would have employed fifty people, from skilled artists, many of them women, to workmen who would fix the kilns.'

'I wonder why the works didn't survive,' Siobhan mused as she looked back up to the stately house. 'I know a lot of china is still made in this region. Limoges will always be famous.'

'Difficulties with the ruling family, the Peydoux family, they say.' Christian's dark eyes looked momentarily sad but briskly he turned away from the disused buildings and beckoned her to follow him back to the house. 'I have made a pot of welcome coffee,' he announced.

She got the feeling that even if he knew the secrets the tumbledown buildings held in their stones this wasn't the time to share them. Perhaps, one day over a bottle of Armagnac to loosen his tongue and make him recall old gossip . . .

Siobhan looked back at the chimney pointing high to the sky, at the cluster of bowed roofs and the forlorn windows of the porcelain works winking in the sunlight.

Then, something flashed at the periphery of her vision. A movement, fleeting, barely there, up at one of the highest windows of the old works. She opened her mouth to point it out, but Christian had strode on. She strained to see more clearly. Was it a reflection of something playing tricks on her? No, she was convinced it was a human face she had glimpsed at the cobwebbed window. Fleetingly there, one moment in sight, gone in the blink of an eye. Pale, doll-like, female.

Siobhan shielded her eyes from the bright sun. It was beginning to get to her. She should have worn sunglasses. The building, when she took a last look back at it, was clearly deserted. The light could play funny tricks and surely no-one would be up in that dusty old place all alone. Had the recent stress she had been under led to her imagining things?

Normally, Siobhan wasn't the sort of girl to imagine anything. Straight 'A's in her exams had been gained by sheer strength of purpose. A career in continuity was only possible for some-one with a sharp mind. She turned away from the red brick building explaining to herself that she'd had a tiring drive, her head was feeling muzzy.

Nevertheless, she glanced back, curiosity drawing her.

There was nothing.

There was no-one.

Who Believes in Ghosts?

They had reached the manor house. Christian took out a bunch of long keys and first unlocked a shutter twice her height. Then he turned the keys in an inner door decorated with stained-glass panes to let them into a grand faded hallway painted eggshell blue.

'This is the heart of the house,' he said with pride. Siobhan realised that although the house wasn't his, he had a proprietorial love of its solid brick and heavy wood, and had been the only one to care for it in years.

'How long have you been looking after La Refuge?'

'Ten years now, man and boy. Isn't that how the English say it? I don't live here all the time. I have family close by who need me. There is a small farm house that comes with the job. But I always sleep here at La Refuge if we have trouble.'

Siobhan's ears pricked up.

'Trouble? What kind of trouble?'

His mouth curved into one of the most attractive smiles she had ever seen. Wide, with perfect chalk white teeth. He should do it more often. She'd noticed he didn't smile readily, and she wondered why. A man this young surely couldn't have so many cares on his shoulders that he had forgotten how to smile.

'Our troubles here in the country are as mundane as a leak in the roof, a burst pipe, mice running about behind the walls. Simple troubles, not something that will need to worry you.'

Siobhan got the sense Christian was trying to make light of something which had more behind it.

'I will of course sleep at La Refuge all the time you are here.'

'Really, you needn't, I don't want to put you out.' Besides, she thought, I don't know you, and you have the sort of eyes which could disturb a girl's sleep.

24

'Do not worry, I shall not impose on you. I know you will be busy working. But an old house has a life of its own, it creaks and sighs from being baked in the sun all day and being chilled at night. This can be unnerving.

'I shall be down in the west wing, just along the passageway if you need me, on the side where the sun sets, and you will be down in the east wing where the sun rises. I will always be within calling distance.

'You shall have the main bedroom to yourself as well as a large en-suite bathroom. I have lit the fire in your room the last few evenings to air it.'

'It sounds delightful.' Siobhan wasn't sure that she needed someone to live in with her, but she was touched at his care and attention.

'I understand from your producer,' Christian continued, 'that the whole of the crew are to live here once the filming starts so I have arranged for the water to be switched on and the lighting to be checked and fixed for safety. This was one of the first dwellings in the area to have electric lights — it was considered state of the art in its day. All the heating is by log fires and I am happy to lay those each morning ready for the evening.'

'Will we really need those in the height of summer?'

'The ceilings are high, and the evenings get cold and damp in a house so close to the river. A house is like a living being. It has needs, and wishes to be warm. This poor house has been neglected and empty for too long. Its passages have missed the running feet of children, its dining-room has longed for the laughter and song of diners enjoying good food cooked with love. Sometimes you can almost hear . . . ' Christian trailed off. 'Sorry, I am letting my imagination run away with me.'

'No, go on.' Siobhan urged him.

'Nothing . . . I meant nothing. It's just that I feel the history in this house, I know something of it from my own studies. I did history at university although I've never had the chance to make it my career. Fate has always kept me here.'

His clipped voice signalled he wanted to say no more as he led her briskly through the hallway to the kitchen. The rooms she glimpsed were under dust sheets, shutters were locked tight against the blinding sun.

When they got to the kitchen she sensed he had been to a great deal of trouble to make it habitable. A large black range had been polished and its brass handles shone. The flagstone floor was newly washed and smelled of cleaning fluid. On the hob a cafetière sat on a trivet and the waft of coffee made her breathe deep.

He served it with warmed milk.

'Cafe au lait, mademoiselle.'

She liked the way his lips curved around the French words, his accent caressing the simplest of phrases making them special. They sat and he looked happy that she had a good appetite.

27

'This is a speciality of the Perigord region, a tart made with walnuts, chestnut flour and butter. It melts in the mouth, yes?'

'It's wonderful, the best I've ever tasted.'

They ate the tart from delicate plates with a turquoise and gold plated rim.

'These were made in the porcelain works. There is a whole set, nearly a hundred pieces,' he announced. 'Now I guess you will want to see the rest of the house.'

'If you don't mind. That coffee's perked me up no end.'

'It's my pleasure.'

As they walked and chatted, it was evident that he loved every room, opening doors with a flourish.

'This is the dining-room. I am looking forward to see it being used in the way it was intended. I have imagined it many a time at its best in the evening with a fire in the grate, the table made up with the silver from this sideboard and the chandelier cleaned and lit. Maybe now you film people are here, the house will look like it did in its heyday.'

As he spoke, Christian uncovered the furniture from its dust sheets. Siobhan helped. They unwrapped a long wooden dining table which, once polished, would have a sheen like glass. Then, 12 high backed chairs with maroon fleur de lys emblems on golden backgrounds emerged from under musty covers and finally a corner desk on delicate legs was revealed.

The parchment-coloured walls were panelled and hand painted with vines, grapes and gold strips. It was like unveiling a sleeping beauty who had been slumbering in a woodland glade underneath a pile of dun-coloured leaves. The house felt as if it were yawning awake and stretching its arms.

'The murals in this house are something very special.' Siobhan ran her hands over round purple grapes, so realistically painted.

'They have been done by an expert.

Rumours are that it was one of the girls who painted the dinner services, and was particularly famed for her depictions of fruit, insects and all things natural, who was commissioned by the owner to produce the wall decorations. They are works of art, aren't they?'

'Yes, so lifelike.' Siobhan was entranced. She couldn't help wondering about the painter. How old would she have been? In those days there were no restrictions on child labour. If a girl could work and if she were as talented as all that she'd have been put to earning money for her family, however young she was.

She'd have had to stand on ladders, craning her neck for hours on end to achieve those wonderful fruits and flowers. She'd have sweated in the heat of summer, and her fingers would have frozen in the depths of winter. What had become of her? Who had loved her? Had she been treated well or badly by the rich owner?

As they walked through the rooms,

Siobhan found her senses overloaded with the personality of the house and the presence of Christian Lavelle. His voice was as resonant as a cello as he recounted brief histories of some of the treasures the house held.

He ran his hands affectionately along carved chair backs and she marvelled at the elegance of his hands, long fingered and lightly callused from honest physical work.

Christian was part of it all. It was as if he had grown magically as a side shoot from one of the giant oaks in the garden, and walked in here taking up residence, like the robust wooden furniture. Each time Christian opened another set of thick long curtains, dust motes whirled crazily in the sunlight as if they were dancing at the prospect of new visitors.

Christian's detailed descriptions, included evocative words such as, 'sconces', 'ormolu' and 'baroque'. Then he turned to her with a look of concern.

'I can see that you are tired by your

flight and I have been droning on endlessly.'

She realised she had been lost in listening to him and had become silent.

'No, not at all. It's just that it's all so opulent, and I can't help thinking that it's going to be extremely hard work getting everything dusted, cleaned and ready in time for the others. They'll be arriving in two weeks and I'll have to have it looking sparkling by then. The house is a dream come true for someone who loves objects like I do. But the amount of work is daunting.'

'I am sorry to have overwhelmed you.' There was that devastating smile again. 'I ought to let you rest before dinner and we can then discuss the practicalities of bringing La Refuge to life. I have one or two ideas but first, come, let us get your car and I will take your cases up to your room.'

As he lugged her cases upstairs, not allowing her to help, she felt she ought to explain.

'I'm sorry my cases are so heavy.

They're not entirely full of clothes — it's my script, a pile of notes and some research books. Sometimes I work online but I wasn't sure of the internet access here.'

'You're right.' He turned at the top of the stairs and made his way down to the end room. 'The internet is a luxury here, the signal comes and goes in such an isolated place. You'll find books more reliable.'

He elbowed a door open to the most delectable bedroom she had ever seen. More of a boudoir. Her eyes were large as saucers.

'You like this room?' His chest puffed out with pride.

'Like it? It's absolutely gorgeous. This must have been the master's bedroom.'

'Indeed it was, and decorated with perfect taste. The four-poster bed has been fully cleaned and made with new Egyptian cotton sheets but the curtains and the swags and tails at the window are all original.'

Siobhan walked in, open-mouthed.

The walls glowed golden yellow and the bed and windows were hung with shot silk. A superb armoire stood in the corner. A rich rug depicting country scenes covered the centre of the floor.

In the opposite corner a chaise longue stood under a mirror in a curled golden frame. Best of all, a beautiful writing desk with its polished surface stood ready for her to spread out her research materials. It was in pride of place under the window looking out on the spreading garden.

'It's such a beautiful room and as clean and neat as a new pin. You must have spent ages getting this ready, Christian. Thank you.'

'It was a pleasure.' He glowed as he motioned her towards the bathroom.

What she saw there made her step back in amazement. It wasn't the two sinks, the massive roll-top bath or the shower in the corner with its antique fixed shower head that amazed her, magnificent though they were. It was the mural on the walls which went all around the room and depicted elegant birds of prey and a perfectly rendered kestrel all painted in a country landscape.

'It's stunning, it's such a privilege to stay here.' She gazed about.

'Good.' Christian nodded his head in approval. 'Dinner will be in,' he consulted his watch, 'an hour and fifteen minutes.'

'I hope you haven't gone to any trouble, a sandwich would be fine.'

But he merely raised an eyebrow as if to say that the idea of having something as mundane as a sandwich was absurd.

'My sister has been shopping and cooking for the past two days. She is more excited than a child with a new toy to have an English guest from the glamorous world of film. She would be totally disappointed not to be able to show off her Perigord specialities. I hope you will have a good appetite?'

'I'll be starving. Budget airlines don't feed you anything nowadays except at an exorbitant cost. I'd love a proper meal after I've taken a bath if that's OK.'

'Please do.' He gave her the slightest of slight bows, bending marginally at the waist in a way that was totally and delightfully Gallic. Then she listened to his steps creaking away through the ancient passage and down the stairs.

What a superb setting this palatial old house was. She felt cocooned in its splendour and an instant love for it spread through her body as she ran her hands across the furnishings. She felt the sheer glory of quality underneath her fingers. In an age of flat-packed furniture, her very soul responded with joy to the glory of things that had been handmade by craftsmen of long ago.

It was as if they talked to her down the ages through the things they had made. They had gained immortality by giving joy long after the hands that had crafted these beautiful things held no more than the fertile earth in their graves.

Siobhan collapsed on to the four-poster and felt its squishy eiderdown wrapping round her like a warm hug. As she lay, she looked at the murals and thought of the girl who painted them. Siobhan closed her eyes, listened to the carolling of birds in the gardens and felt suddenly dozy. Five minutes, that's all she needed, a nap before she ran her bath. She let her body succumb to slumber. Felt herself happily drift away until, at the other-worldly half-conscious point between wakefulness and sleeping she was aware of one of her senses being teased. Was she dreaming?

In the far distance, perhaps coming to her ears through time rather than space, she could hear a swishing, gentle, rhythmic brushing, not unlike a cloth being wiped over a surface. In her mind's eye, the ghostly half-seen face at the window floated before her.

She imagined the girl who had painted the walls in the room she now lay in, in her dreamlike state, washing the walls, wiping them of dust ready to paint. The sound, swish, swish, swish, lulled her but also somewhere in her rational mind, scared her. Siobhan felt a presence in the room.

With a start and a terrific jolt, she woke, sitting up straight as a poker. Her heart thumped. But there, in the corner was nothing more sinister than two gold-green eyes in the fluffiest, cutest face of a long-haired black kitten.

Somewhere on the way up here, the tiny animal had picked up a dried oak leaf on its tail. As the tail swished from side to side, Siobhan realised what had made the unearthly noise which had fired her imagination.

'You're not a ghost at all.' She eased herself off the bed picking up the kitten, delighting in its soft fur. 'You naughty thing, you gave me such a fright. We don't believe in ghosts, do we?'

Then, she picked off the troublesome leaf and deposited the feline outside her door to scamper off down the passage, its tiny legs galloping. She chuckled at her own over active imagination as she went off to run her bath. Nevertheless, even now, she didn't feel alone.

An Icy Chill

The meal was superb, chunky farm-house pate on walnut bread to start, a cassoulet with haricot beans and duck followed by the smoothest of crème brûlée with bitter espresso. Christian had produced a bottle of Arnaud & Fils Cabernet d'Anjou which had slipped down as sweet as honey to accompany a creamy chevre and home-baked oat biscuits.

Siobhan was introduced to Janique, Christian's younger sister, who hovered around like a waitress on her first day and had to be told gently by Christian to sit and relax with them.

'Janique is a twin and loves to cook. Her sister, Mariette, is off with a new boyfriend this evening. But, if you are agreeable, the two of them have volunteered to take on the task of cleaning and getting the house spruced up.

'They have both finished college just this last week so are at a loose end. They are learning English along with their degrees, one in architecture, the other in design. They would like to practise their English on you while they work. Is that acceptable?'

'That would be ideal, if it suits them.'

Janique nodded shyly and when Siobhan said she'd pay them a respectable hourly rate, the girl's eyes lit up.

'Janique,' Christian said, 'you could start to practise your English on Siobhan now.'

Janique shook her head, laughing as she collected up the dishes and went off to wash them.

Christian shrugged.

'She wants to buy a car,' he continued, 'and learn to drive. She will work very hard if it means her dream of having her own transport comes closer.'

'I don't need hard labour, but I'd love to have the help of her and her sister. When can they start?'

'As soon as possible.'

'Tomorrow, then, the sooner the better. Will they stay at the house too?' At this, Janique who was wiping crumbs off the table, looked concerned, and Siobhan saw her shake her head briskly at Christian.

'Janique's only ever stayed one night, and she won't stay again.'

'Why not?'

The siblings exchanged a look, and Janique clattered around at the huge butler's sink.

'She finds it . . . ' He seemed to struggle to find the right word and Siobhan had the notion that there was more behind the girl's reluctance than he wanted to give away.

'She finds it daunting.' He hesitated. 'It's too big. Our own little farmhouse which has always been the province of the estate manager is tiny by comparison, with lower ceilings and a market garden surrounded by a wall. It is cosy, whereas in this big house . . . Janique feels she rolls around like a chickpea on a plate.'

Siobhan regretted that they would be saying goodbye to Janique each night. She was a pretty little raven-haired thing with generous eyes and a caring air. Siobhan wondered that any nineteen-year-old would pass up the chance to stay in such a romantic house where you could dream that you were lady of the manor. But she shrugged and accepted that for a young girl it didn't hold the attraction of history it did for her.

'I have to walk Janique back home now. It is five minutes down the lane towards the chimney of the old porcelain works. I have made up a fire in the dining-room and Janique has vacuumed and dusted the chairs. Take your wine and cheese wherever you feel most comfortable. I will be back shortly.'

Siobhan watched them from the kitchen window as they walked down the ancient stone steps, and noted before they were sucked into the inky blackness how Christian looked back and waved, checking she was OK.

As she stood, sipping coffee, Siobhan was struck by how different the night was here than from her flat in London. There it never got really dark. Street lamps and car headlights gave out light pollution. Here, the blackness was like a velvet cloak lying over the pine trees in the forest.

Suddenly, Siobhan became aware of how very alone she was. The jolly chatter of her companions had filled the kitchen only a moment ago. But now it felt eerily big, with too much space at her back. She turned and for a fleeting second had the strange notion someone was watching her.

Her eyes darted around the kitchen and she felt her breath come in short bursts. A blip of anxiety welled up. She remembered her yoga classes back home, remembered her gentle Japanese teacher Miroko telling her pupils to 'breathe in for five, then hold for five, then out for five. Whenever you feel uneasy or stressed, breathe like this for a couple of minutes and I guarantee you will ground yourself, you will gain peace'.

Siobhan did as she'd been taught. She had used the technique on crowded trains and when aircraft had been buffeted by turbulence.

She felt herself calming down. There's no-one here skulking in the shadows, there's just you and the black kitten sitting on the chair, and Christian will be back shortly.

Nevertheless, she felt exposed with the shutters at the windows still open, and outside a yawning black void. Siobhan had a yearning to find a room where she could pull the curtains and shut out the darkness. She picked up a tray and loaded her coffee, glass of wine and the last of her plate of biscuits and cheese which was too delicious to leave.

The dining-room felt much cosier and much . . . safer. Was that the right word? Had she felt unsafe? She rationalised all her feelings of vulnerability. It was just that things were changing. Being on edge was understandable.

A fire danced in the grate of the grand dining-room. A table lamp and candles had been lit, making the whole look like a sepia photograph. She took her things off the tray and stood and admired the set-up — it would be absolutely perfect for one of the main scenes in the film, set a week or two before Hallowe'en, where the Edwardian family are sitting down to an anniversary dinner.

Revelations and secrets unfold with the actors in evening dress, and candles reflecting off the polished table. It would have the air of warmth needed to set the scene and contrast it with the drama to follow.

A thrill shot through Siobhan as with her professional eye, she tried to forget her unease and focus instead on the treasures in the room they could use as props. Red leather-bound books with gold lettering, cut-glass decanters. Candlesticks with long glass droplets which tinkled and chimed like a child's toy.

Then she looked up at the paintings on the wall. Many were unremarkable, but as she walked along, one caught her eye. It was of a beautiful young woman who lay, seemingly asleep, in a rowing boat floating down a river.

Siobhan recognised the banks of the river as the Lisle which ran at the bottom of the garden of La Refuge. She had walked down there today with Christian. True, the area was now more overgrown but the vegetation was similar and in the distant background of the painting she could see the weir and the white water beyond.

The girl's blonde hair was festooned with wild blossoms, cornflowers, butter-cups and poppies. The vibrant colours only served to highlight the paleness of her skin and the pristine whiteness of her long muslin dress. The girl looked vulnerable, sleeping as she did — but was she sleeping, or was her state something more sinister?

It was one of the most wonderful

paintings Siobhan had ever seen, so skilfully executed, so totally lifelike that she had the urge to reach out and touch the canvas. It was as if she wanted to reassure herself that the ethereally beautiful skin was warm to the touch and not, heaven forbid, cold and lifeless.

Siobhan peered closer, raising her hand with trepidation. As she moved her forefinger towards the canvas, she suddenly felt an icy chill pass over her limbs, starting at her feet, encroaching on her calves, engulfing her thighs. The cold which crept up from the floor smothering her in dampness was like stepping into an industrial freezer, intense, icy and so immediate it made all the hairs on her body spring to attention. The chill took Siobhan's breath away.

She dropped her hand and shot back from the painting so sharply that she bumped into one of the dining-room chairs, losing her balance.

'Careful there.' Christian came from behind her and she felt his capable grip catch and steady her. She had been so absorbed by the painting and so shocked by the alien rush of dank swampy air that she hadn't heard him return.

Instantly, from feeling icy, she now felt warm, her cheeks burning at his proximity. The pressure points where he had placed a firm grip on her arms were super-sensitised. She was struck by his deep compassionate eyes, the furrow at the centre of his forehead signalling concern. Had he felt that damp chill, too?

She longed to relax into Christian's hold, let him take the weight and save her the trouble of having to stiffen her legs and stand on her own two feet. But she could never do that. It was too alien to yield to another man's arms when so recently the only male embrace she had felt comfortable with had been her fiancé's. Besides, as soon as he'd steadied her, Christian had done the gentlemanly thing and taken a step backwards.

'Are you OK?'

'Yes, yes, of course. It's only that — well, I felt something strange.'

His brows knitted.

'What do you mean?'

It was too difficult to put into words. He looked like the practical sort, strong as a tree, fiercely of the moment. He'd think she was crazy going on about feelings and notions of things which weren't there. The explosion of emotion that had emanated from the painting was so weird.

The concern Siobhan had felt deep in her gut for the girl's welfare sounded ridiculous now she searched for a way to describe it.

And the freezing cold sensation, not like a draught from an open window but more a seeping, all encompassing presence. Something sad, and over-whelmingly tragic had struck Siobhan's soul, and for a moment buried itself under her skin. The overall sensation was something she couldn't explain. 'The crazy English girl' was not

49

something she wanted people to think of her.

'Nothing, really it's nothing. Just a bit of homesickness, perhaps.' She brushed off the incident lightly and walked back to the table, holding the stem of her glass too tightly. 'I'm just not used to being in countryside so silent and in a house so large.'

Christian looked at her quizzically. There was a pregnant pause, as if he wished she'd said more, but he was too polite to push her.

'I am glad now that I decided to stay here. Janique has Mariette and our mother for company. I will be in La Refuge in case you feel something 'strange' again. If there is anything you want, do not hesitate to knock. Maybe now it is time to turn in?'

'Absolutely,' Siobhan said. 'I'm shattered, it's been a long day. Thank you for catching me.' She giggled, and immediately regretted sounding so silly and girlish.

He nodded.

'It's nothing. I hope you sleep well. I will see you tomorrow.'

She wished Christian a very good night, thanked him for a perfect welcome to La Refuge and made her way upstairs.

Tired as she was, it was always Siobhan's rule to get unpacked immediately, her orderly mind needing to find a home for everything. She purposely didn't look out of the windows as she pulled first the outside shutters, then the heavy curtains tightly closed.

All the incidents earlier, she told herself as she hung up trousers and skirts, scarves and dresses, could be easily explained. Her suitcase gradually emptied as she pondered.

It was nonsense to think she had seen a face at the window of the old building, it was just a play of light on the glass. And just now, that feeling of chill must have been no more than a draught from ill-fitting windows. And the feeling of dampness? There was water all around. The old floorboards, the thick beams and rafters in the house were bound to take in the moisture during the day and then breathe it out at night, like a giant at rest — that was the explanation for that.

This house was very old whereas her London flat was new, double glazed, close carpeted and not prone to draughts or subject to the elements. Her flat was merely a box — a very nice one with modern features, downlights and sleek chrome fittings. But she had never thought of it as having a personality or a life of its own. La Refuge, on the other hand, lived and breathed like a person.

Now that she lay in bed, tucked up in lavender-scented sheets in the blackness, it was as if the house sighed and turned in its sleep.

The heat of the day had given way to the chilly small hours and every now and then there was a creak as a joist contracted like weary ancient bones, and settled into stillness.

Outside, an owl hooted and another called to it over the hills. In a moment there was an entire owly conversation going on as they gossiped through the trees. The sound made Siobhan smile and she turned on her side and curled into a ball.

There was nothing to worry about, nothing to cause her concern. The house was just different, huge and monumental, full of the echoes of all the people who had lived here, their hopes and fears, their joy and tears. And she could almost feel their memories reaching out to her from the walls as she drifted into a deep, solid slumber.

Dark Secrets

The next day, Janique turned up on the doorstep, a huge grin on her face, together with her sister Mariette who shook Siobhan's hand with less enthusiasm. They had brought buckets, dusters, polish, brooms, a hoover and rubber gloves. Although Mariette sighed and pouted a lot, the two looked ready for action.

'Where do we start?' Janique asked.

'Oh, I guess in the lounge would be a good place.'

The two girls set to at once. They threw open the shutters and let in the fresh morning air. They carried dust sheets to the patio and giggled and tweeted like hopping French birds as they shook the dust of ages out in the breeze.

They polished the windows with a solution of water, lemon juice and cider vinegar until the glass sparkled like crystal. They hoovered the dusty old floorboards with all the vigour only teenagers hopeful of folding money in their pockets can muster.

Mariette did a lot of sneezing and shook her duster out on the terrace with her nose turned up in disgust. But to be fair, even though it was plain she would rather be schmoozing with her boyfriend, she worked as hard as her sister. She just made sure everyone knew about it, complaining at each new task.

The twins couldn't have been more different in attitude. As the two girls climbed up on ladders and swept away cobwebs from the ceilings with long-handled brooms, Siobhan went through the drawers looking for treasures and scribbling notes about them in a moleskin notebook.

In a couple of hours she had listed knives and forks, bonbon dishes, old photographs and other items.

'How are my sisters doing?' Christian's entry into the room caused the girls to light up as they chattered animatedly in French to him. Mariette, bottom lip protruding, produced a small cut on her finger where it had come into contact with a splinter.

With all the care of a surgeon, he took out of his pocket a small pouch containing tweezers and a mini-medical kit. In a moment, he had removed the splinter, cleaned the finger, applied a plaster and peace was restored.

Then he went off to collect and deliver two hefty baskets of logs and some kindling into the grate. Mariette, seeking more attention, now stomped about and complained of a broken nail, and Janique proudly showed him how beautifully the silver on the frame of an old mirror had polished up. When he gently removed a cobweb from Mariette's hair, she shrieked and he laughed at her conceit.

'This isn't really Mariette's idea of fun, is it, my darling? What's more, you should both be trying to speak English while you have an expert here.' He winked at Siobhan and she felt her knees go weak despite herself.

'*Non*. I am not made for this sort of work, everything is so feelthy.' Mariette's expressive eyes flashed like green topaz. 'One day I will show you all by leaving here and doing something very . . . very . . . ' Her English failed her.

'I'm sure you will.' Christian looked at her indulgently. 'But while we are waiting for this amazing event, perhaps you would go and make us all a nice coffee.'

'Wiz plesir.' She threw down her rubber gloves. 'I would rather be a bartender . . . '

'Probably more like waitress,' Siobhan interrupted.

' . . . Zan a cleaner any day.' Mariette flounced off.

Janique shrugged, not at all bothered with hard work.

'I will finish the window-doors. How do you say these in English, Siobhan?'

'Well, actually, we always call them French windows.'

'That's right, I must remember. They are good looking, yes?'

'Yes, they're looking great and you're both working so hard. This room is really beginning to glow, isn't it, especially in the morning sunlight? It's beginning to get hot — crikey, I didn't realise it was nearly noon.'

'It is my favourite room.' Christian ran his hand across a newly polished writing bureau and breathed the scent of lavender furniture polish deep into his lungs.

'It is nice to see the ash and oak come alive — the furniture has been dry and hungry all these years.'

'Why on earth doesn't the man who owns La Refuge enjoy this house?'

Christian slumped down into one of the newly cleaned sofas and put his head in his hands. For a moment, Siobhan was worried about him. He had not appeared to her to be a man who let much trouble him.

But mention of the owner had made his shoulders drop, and she noticed that Janique now hovered next to Christian.

'Monsieur Pierre Seydoux, the man who owns La Refuge, has no soul. Sad to say he is a very buttoned up man. He has no children, no grandchildren or wife, so even though he is rich in money he is poor in the things that make a man whole.

'He inherited La Refuge with a number of other properties from his wealthy grandfather. He stayed here briefly one summer in the 1950s as a young man and occasionally returns for family reasons.

'But he has never been interested in this house or the area. It is too quiet for him and too far away from the bright lights of the big city. He saw this house only as a possible playground for him and his rich friends. He is a thoughtless man who has had more than one run-in with the people of Thiviers.

'My own mother is just one of the people he has crossed. With all his money he could do so much good, but he cannot see beyond his own nose. The other year he had a swimming pool built in the grounds thinking he might use this as a holiday home. I was dreading him returning. My mother has not been well and knowing he was back in the area would not have helped her recovery.'

'I'm sorry to hear that.'

'Then, when he did come here he only stayed a week. It is typical of him to come around and disturb things before deciding it was not for him and wanting to sell.'

'I wonder why that was. It's such a beautiful place.'

'Siobhan, I must tell you that there have always been rumours and stories about this house among the locals. You have heard it said La Refuge is haunted.'

'I have but I don't believe in that sort of thing.'

'Well, while Pierre Seydoux was here, he was scared out of his wits. It might just have been his conscience. But he said there was something evil here. Rich families often have tragedies surrounding them. Pierre Seydoux's ancestors were not kind people. They were unscrupulous, there are rumours of wrongs done.'

At that point, Janique moved towards Christian. She placed a hand over his hands which had become balled into white knuckled fists in his lap. Janique's wide eyes seemed to plead to Siobhan to ask no further questions and Siobhan was suddenly certain in the knowledge that Christian suspected more than he was prepared to tell.

As if she needed to do something to distract him, Janique piped up.

'Christian, coffee has arrived, and Mariette has brought marzipan and sugared bonbons, too.' She poured a strong black one for him as Mariette placed down the tray, and helped him to a generous portion of the marzipan which had been fashioned into realistic fruits. He relaxed a little and it was as if a storm cloud had passed. He got up and wandered over to the fireplace.

'Then, of course, your film company got wind of the fact that an old house and its contents which hadn't been touched since the end of the nineteenth century was up for sale and they asked him if they could use it before it went on the market.

'Pierre Seydoux has always had an eye for the main chance and could see that not only would you film people clean everything up but that also your film would give the house a cachet which would increase its market value. Market value is something he has always understood.'

'You hold this house in such high regard it seems a shame for there to be tensions,' Siobhan said.

'He is the sort of person who sees everything in terms of his own advantage. He only keeps me on because he knows how fond I am of this house and its grounds and that I will not leave the area because my mother is here.

'It makes me a reliable guardian of

his property. His father and his grandfather were the same — they used people. They are a family with something rotten at their core.'

Who, Siobhan wondered, did Christian have to help him through these problems? Obviously the twins were a comfort to him, but he seemed to be caring for them as well as his mother.

'Still.' He brightened, walking over to the sweetmeats, popping a couple of marzipan in his mouth and washing them down with bitter coffee. 'I love this house, and at least until it is sold, we can be in it and enjoy having you here. What I will do when we have to leave I don't know.

'Will you allow me to help you sort through things? I have not yet shown you the secret cupboards in the hall. They hold many treasures.'

Siobhan was glad he had perked up. She didn't like to see his brown eyes looking wistful. At heart he was a positive person.

'I'd be delighted. There's nothing

more intriguing than a secret cup-board.'

'Come then.' They left the two girls to finish off the lounge and Christian opened both the front and the back French windows which led off the dual facing hallway.

The hall had a character all of its own. In the centre was a round ebony table which the girls had filled with a vase spilling over with stems of lacy hydrangeas in azure and cream. The hall was lined in eggshell blue panels, perfectly setting off the sofa and chair which stood there ready for the use of newly entered guests. Upholstered in jolly navy and white toile de jouie material depicting shepherdesses and the French hills and valleys, there couldn't have been a more welcoming space.

Siobhan watched in anticipation as Christian ran his hand down one of the doors, to exactly the right spot and, like a magician pulling a rabbit out of a hat, pressed it sharply. The mechanism clicked and the panel shot out to reveal a door to a separate cupboard.

'Every one of these panels hides its own cupboard,' he said, 'and each holds its own treasures.'

Siobhan shook her head in disbelief.

'This house is like a box of delights. I can see why you love it so much.'

'Indeed, it is unique.' He gave her a long, intense look. 'La Refuge is like the most fascinating of women, many layered, endlessly intriguing, a constant joy.' Then his face became serious. 'But with secrets hidden very deep, and some of them dark. Family secrets are the worst.'

She looked at him curiously. Christian, she realised, felt the weight of the secrets of the past and unless they were uncovered and put to rest, he could not be free to enjoy life unconditionally. Did he feel he was bearing some guilt? To know that a wrong has been done and not be able to right it must be a terrible thing. She got the sense that behind his slightly stern Gallic exterior was a man who could experience great joy but that this was constrained.

He was a man in chains, his spirit clipped, his joy and desire bound with a heavy heart. If only, Siobhan thought, someone could find out the truth of this house and the secrets it held, it would lay the past to rest and help Christian enjoy the present and the future.

Might she be the one to do that for him? Perhaps someone with fresh eyes and with a woman's intuition might be able to help Christian and she so desperately wanted to.

She wished he could trust her with his concerns. Yet again, she observed his delight in the house's treasures as he took the contents of the cupboard out and lay them on the ebony table.

It was a collection of linen, superb lace tablecloths no doubt wrought by hand and involving hours of painstaking work by expert seamstresses. Snowy white napkins were carefully wrapped in tissue papers to shield them from the elements.

'Aren't they beautiful?' Christian smoothed his hands across them. He studied the tablecloth intently then found what he was looking for as he showed her two opposing corners.

'See here, this large set of embroidered letters is the grand monogram of the person for whom the tablecloth was made. But here, hidden in the corner and worked to look like the centre of a flower, is another set of initials. These would have been the way the lady who worked the cloth would have stamped her mark on it. She has secretly woven her own initials into it, making it for ever as much hers as the rich person who commissioned it. They had spirit, those women.'

As he spoke, he looked wistful.

'There are defining moments in all our lives, are there not? When I was eighteen, I took myself to the Greek islands. I had no money, but a head full of dreams and a romantic nature that cared nothing for practicalities. I worked my way overland doing odd jobs, starving on occasions with no money and falling upon people's generosity.

'Thank heaven the Greeks are a generous people and they saw my ribs poking through my clothes and often gave me bread, olives and honey. One day, when I had just finished a large job cutting wood and finally had some coins in my pocket, I was sitting at a bar in Crete enjoying a coffee and a glass of iced water. It was after a hearty meal of fried fish caught fresh from the bay. It was near Elounda, very close to the island of Spinalonga which was a leper colony right up until the Fifties.

'An old lady appeared. She was the most ancient person I had ever seen, her face creased with the sun, like tissue paper, but beautiful still, for all the years she had seen had etched themselves on her skin in a wonderful panorama of experience and wisdom.

'Her hair was white as a dove, and plaited. The braids were wound round her head, she was the picture of neatness.

'At first I thought she was begging and I put my hand in my pocket to give her the last of my money. Her back was bent over and she was dressed entirely in black and I noticed there was a patch in the side of her dress where it had been mended but she still took pride in her appearance.

'As she came closer though, I saw she was approaching people trying to sell something. Draped across her arm was a lace tablecloth not unlike this one.

'Tourists were waving her away and I felt so sorry for her because it was obviously something she had put a huge amount of work into. It may even have been something she didn't want to part with but had been forced into by circumstances. I so wanted to buy it from her but I had nothing like a decent price to offer her.

'Unlike the poor old woman however, I had my youth and my strength and many years before me. I took her hand and pressed into it all the money I had — it wasn't much but it was something.

'She held out her arm to offer me the beautiful tablecloth but I wouldn't have dreamed of taking it, it was worth far more than I had. I often wonder if she ever managed to sell it and if she did whether she was given a decent price.

'Whenever I look at this beautiful tablecloth, I think of her, of her strength and resilience. Women throughout history have had to stay at home to look after their children and have worked like slaves in their own houses.'

'You're so right, Christian,' Siobhan said, with a new and deeper respect for him. A sensitive man was a wonderful thing and so different from her fiancé Gerrard.

'I'm lucky I've been born in this era where I can do any job I want, I've read of women in Victorian London who prepared rabbit skins in their own homes and got lung diseases from the fluff they breathed in.

'Then there were women who made beautiful silk flowers to adorn the hats of wealthy society ladies while they struggled to earn pennies, their fingers burned by the hot irons they used to curl the petals.'

'That's why I am passionate for Janique and Mariette to continue their studies and have as many chances in life as possible. Living here, my being paid a reasonable wage but most of all having the cheap accommodation of the farmhouse allows me to get them through university.

'It is a must that they finish their studies. Now, let me show you the other cupboards.'

One revealed glasses and decanters tooled with vine leaves and another held a superb collection of kid leather gloves with seed pearl buttons. But the best held a superb collection of china. He handed her a cup. It felt like an eggshell sitting in her hand.

'What beautiful workmanship,' she

said. 'These pieces must all be hand-painted, you can see the brush strokes on the daisies and buttercups, and look how superbly executed these blue flowers are.'

Christian took it gently from Siobhan, and as he did so, his hand brushed hers. She felt the slight roughness of it, the warmth, the strength in the muscles and sinews. She was acutely aware of his closeness as a rush of adrenalin shot through her veins. The two of them stood as if in their own bubble, enjoying the beautiful objects together. Christian knew so many things, and he felt deeply and observed minutely. A man like that could never be boring.

'If you hold good porcelain up to the sun,' he told her, 'you can see the light shining through it.'

'It's wonderful.'

'These are indeed little works of art. This whole service was painted by one girl at the factory, Marie-Louise Thizy, a local girl who was turning into quite a star. People were asking specifically for her to produce whole dinner services like this and set pieces like large flower vases. Until she disappeared.'

Mystery in Paradise

Siobhan put down the cup.

'Disappeared?'

'No-one knows what happened to her. A search took place, the whole of Thiviers was involved. Men scoured the fields with pitchforks. They took dogs out to the woods, and horseback riders covered every inch of the surrounding hills. The mayor set up search parties of people's homes and a string of suspects was brought in and then released.

'Rumours abounded and it caused nastiness in the village. These small places have their own codes and it was believed that people who had grudges against certain of their male neighbours put out stories that they were to blame, in an effort to pay off old scores.

'But none of this came to anything. It was as if she had been spirited off the earth. The river was dredged but nothing was ever found.

'In the end it was thought Marie-Louise had run away. Sad to say, a lot of jewellery disappeared from this house the day she went. People assumed she had taken it, but anyone could have stolen it and it could just be a coincidence.

'Marie-Louise was a girl of good character. What's more, she was becoming famed for her work and earning good money. Her pay was put up because she worked so hard and her painting was exceptional. She had no need to steal. And she did not work in the house but in the factory.

'I don't see how a girl like that could have broken in. The house would have been thoroughly shuttered and locked and they would have had guard dogs. She wasn't one of the servants at La Refuge, so she wouldn't have had access to it. A tragedy and a great miscarriage of justice has taken place here, if only these walls could reveal their secrets.'

Christian looked suddenly grave.

'Marie-Louise was a distant relative of mine — her blood runs through my veins. A wrong was done to her and that is a wound to my family. For years I have wanted to solve the mystery. For one so innocent, who created such beauty, to have been wronged is an affront to decency.

'After she had gone, some beautiful paintings were found hidden in a storeroom in the factory where she kept her brushes. They were removed and packed up and stored in the attic here. I could not bear to think of them gathering dust, unseen and unloved.

'Pierre Seydoux, the owner of this house, had clearly hidden them in an attempt to make people forget her. There are rumours he went round Thiviers and bought up all the books in which her works were mentioned. The ones in the library in town even became 'lost'. He wanted her memory expunged.

'Now why would he do that if he didn't suspect something? There is no doubt his ancestor was involved in her disappearance.'

'But what would Pierre Seydoux think if he came back to La Refuge and found you had hung up all her paintings?' Siobhan asked.

'Someone has to defend the innocent. I do not care about his sensitivities. Besides, he will not come here again, he hates La Refuge as much as I love it.

'As well as those paintings which I have dotted around the house, there is also a mural by her on one of the walls in the guest bedrooms. It is a rural scene with hills and meadows and woodland flowers. It is clearly her style, exactly like she painted on her pieces of porcelain.

'If you look closely at the mural, you will see there is a charming figure of a girl, leading a goat on a little pink rope. She is taking it down to a pond to drink. The girl is beautiful with long waving hair and a serene smile, like an angel.

'It is clearly a self-portrait. She must have painted it when she was very happy and I think she painted it for someone in the house, perhaps someone she was in love with.

'When I found her paintings which Pierre Seydoux had shut away, I was incensed. I am hoping that having the paintings featured in your film will see a revival of her memory, it could be a rebirth for Marie-Louise.

'You were looking at one of her paintings last night when I came into the lounge, of a young girl lying in a boat surrounded by flowers. That was her.'

'Ah.' Siobhan felt an immediate affinity with Marie-Louise Thizy. Siobhan was artistic and hard working. She had made her own way in life, had used her talents productively, just like Marie-Louise.

But Siobhan lived in a different age, one where a woman was safer and could be independent and not done down by a lord of the manor.

'I must go and see the mural at some point. There are so many bedrooms, and I've only been in my own and one or two others just to pick up objects which might be useful for the film.'

Siobhan had been enchanted by the girl in the boat. She would never have imagined it was a self-portrait — it was such an odd pose for that, but so calm. Why should Marie-Louise paint herself as if she were asleep?

Or perhaps, Siobhan thought with a shiver, as if she were dead? Had she realised her future was precarious? And why would a girl who was doing so well simply up and disappear? That seemed unlikely.

Siobhan lifted the porcelain again, and held it to the sunlight. As she did so, a strange thing happened. Though it was a still day, a sudden draught of air gusted from the open French windows at the back of the house to the front.

In doing so, it brought in a cloud of

hydrangea blossom, little rounded florets of powder blue and white rolling in like ping-pong balls sent by an invisible hand across the polished floor to land at Siobhan's feet.

She bent down, picked one up and gasped. There on one of the lily white petals was a moist spot of deep, angry vermillion red. Siobhan immediately dropped the blossom as if she had been pricked by a thorn.

'What is it?' Christian, protective as ever, came to her side and picked up the blossom. He held it in his palm. The livid spot stained his finger an ugly crimson.

'It's blood.' Siobhan felt her stomach lurch. 'It . . . it's a message, like a sign, as if someone, somewhere is trying to communicate with us.' She looked over to where the blossoms had rolled.

Christian moved swiftly towards the window, stirring the motes of dust swirling in the sunshine. The two of them stepped out of the French windows to investigate and peered round the balustraded patio.

There was no-one there. Apart from the birds singing and the bees buzzing, all was calm. Just a late summer's day. Suddenly there was a quiet chirrup, a guilty-sounding miaow.

'Oh,' Christian said. 'That is all it was, just our wildlife playing tricks.'

There was the fluffy black kitten Siobhan had encountered the day before, and around her played three gorgeous siblings, mischievous but deadly balls of fluff.

Mama cat was showing her kittens how to hunt and a poor mouse lay dead, its tiny legs curled in the air, a small trail of blood marking the stone of the patio.

With care, using a spade leaning up against the patio, Christian dug a hole and tipped the pathetic corpse into it, much to the chagrin of the cats who loped off in disgust.

'That's nature,' Christian said. 'In their frenzy, the kittens must have detached some of the blossoms.'

'But Christian, there's no wind at all today. What blew the flowers into the house? How could that have happened? See, over there, at the end of the garden?' Someone on the adjacent land had lit a bonfire.

'Those wisps of smoke are going nowhere. There hasn't been a whiff of wind all morning.'

'I do not know.'

'Christian, you're not a good liar. I reckon you do know. I think the rumours of a ghost here aren't just fantasy and idle speculation. I think people have seen and felt things over the years, and you've probably seen and felt more than most.'

This was what Christian had kept hidden from her. His absolute love for the house had caused him to be cautious when anyone mentioned spirits and the like. She guessed the last thing he wanted was unwelcome visitors, kids, teenagers who might break in on the nights the house was empty to find out if the rumours were true.

He might actually be very worried about the effect the film being made here might have on the future of the house but he was such a gentleman, he had welcomed her and looked after her despite that.

She then related to him the feeling she had had standing looking at Marie-Louise's painting the night before. He nodded his head.

'I, too, have had the same sensation,' he admitted, 'but I didn't want to frighten you. But now we are talking about it, I will say that though I have seen and felt many things in this house, I have never felt that the spirit who haunts it is malevolent. Just deeply troubled.'

Siobhan sat down under the cream sun umbrella on one of the original wrought iron garden chairs and rubbed her hand on the arm.

'If only these inanimate objects could talk to us, Christian, they could tell us the truth. They could tell us what happened to Marie-Louise. I feel it is her ghost which haunts this house.

'I sensed last night, an overwhelming presence, not of evil but of sadness and a need to put things right. It is as if she cannot rest.'

'I feel it, too, most acutely,' he answered. 'I carry the weight of the injustice that was done to her on my own shoulders because I am here in this house, and like a jewel casket, the house I am sure holds her secret somewhere if only we could unlock it.'

'And not just the house but also the old porcelain works — maybe there are clues there,' Siobhan said. 'Would you show me round some time?'

'It has been shut up for years. I only go in occasionally just to check all is well, but I will show it to you while you are here. Maybe tomorrow.'

'I'd like that.'

Christian gave her one of his beaming smiles, the sort of smile which only came to light periodically. As he did so, the trio of kittens came dashing round the corner, fighting over a leaf, paws everywhere, fluffy tails like ostrich feathers plumed in the air.

It gave Siobhan and Christian a good laugh and truly Siobhan felt as if this could be a paradise on earth if only they could solve Marie-Louise's mystery.

Plea from the Past

The next day, Siobhan was excited at the thought of going around the old porcelain works. She'd arranged it with Christian for after lunch. This morning, Christian was busy. He had booked in a local pool maintenance man to have the pool serviced so it would be up and running for when all the actors, actresses and other film people were due to arrive in two weeks' time.

The film was a time-slip story set partly in the present day where there was to be a big pool party scene with lots of beautiful people, and partly in the past when the house and inhabitants were quite different.

Siobhan also knew that one of the lures for getting an up and coming model turned actress to accept the film's main female lead was the possibility of staying in such a beautiful location and sampling all the top restaurants in the region.

The actress, Philadelphia Grant, was getting a reputation as a diva and Siobhan wasn't looking forward to her arrival in a fortnight's time. Utterly stunning, and still only twenty, Siobhan understood the model's ultimate goal had always been to break into films. Such driving ambition in one so very young was something which Siobhan found daunting.

Siobhan, Christian and his sisters were enjoying breakfast on the patio together. Croissant and baguettes which Mariette had been persuaded to cycle into Thiviers to collect, liberally spread with butter and Janique's homemade apricot jam, had been washed down with a large cafetière of heart-stoppingly strong coffee. It was a breakfast made in heaven.

'That was delicious, thank you.' Siobhan licked her fingers. 'If I had breakfast like that every day I'd be as huge as this house.'

'But you are so sleem,' Mariette,

voluptuous and curvy, looked envious. 'I cannot think that will ever 'appen.'

'Only because with my job I find it difficult to find time to eat. I should eat more healthily.'

Christian was pouring her a third cup of the delicious coffee when Siobhan's mobile phone went. Her relaxed mood changed immediately as she saw the name of the caller come up. Gerrard. What on earth did he want?

Her heart did a somersault. Could it be possible she still had feelings for him? She'd have said a resounding no. But the heart is a strange thing. She got up from her seat and made her way across towards the flower-beds, away from the ears of the others.

'Gerrard?'

'Siobhan? Glad I caught you. I've been trying to pluck up the courage to speak to you for days. Are you OK?'

'Yes. Are you? Why are you phoning me Gerrard, after all that's happened? I . . . I'm really busy at the moment. I'm working. In France.'

For the last few days, she'd also been blissfully untroubled by all the trauma of their cancelled wedding. It had been nice to have something else to think about. All that was behind her now and she didn't want Gerrard digging things up again.

'Yes, I know you're working in France, Siobhan, that's why I phoned you. I'm here, too.'

'What?' she nearly yelled. 'Why are you in France?'

'Working — near Thiviers, actually.'

Gerrard worked in wealth management. He had clients and contacts all around the world and often went away. What a coincidence though, Siobhan thought, that he should be here, not a million miles away from where she was.

'I'm staying in a hotel. I thought I'd come over and see you.'

'Why?'

'I've got a free afternoon. I'll pop round. I need to see you, Siobhan. Please, please listen to me . . . '

'Gerrard, no, I'm sorry, it's not convenient.'

'Only for a short while, Siobhan. Please, don't be cruel. We don't hate each other, do we? We didn't split acrimoniously. I wasn't unfaithful or anything. I miss you.

'Look, I've got to go, I've got a conference call in two minutes. It's La Refuge you're at, isn't it? I looked it up on the net.

'I like an old house — remember how we used to go round them together? Anyhow, I'll see you later.'

With that, he'd rung off before she could tell him he had no right to invade her life again. She jabbed the phone digits trying to call him back but it went to answerphone.

That was always Gerrard's problem, he didn't understand the word no. That's why they'd split up, and she hadn't been able to go through with the wedding.

The conversation she'd just had encompassed Gerrard in a nutshell. He was a bull in a china shop when it came to relationships.

At first when they'd started going out, she'd been totally bowled over. He was fantastically caring, flattering, always had her best interests at heart. He was the most attentive boyfriend she'd ever had. Friends told her how lucky she was.

'Isn't Gerrard adorable. I wish my boyfriend would buy me flowers like that. And he's so focused on everything you need, opening doors for you, pulling your chair out when you sit down. He never takes his eyes off you.'

He was always asking how she was, always totally in tune with what she liked. She'd only have to mention in passing that lobster was her favourite and the next weekend he'd have booked them in to the best London restaurant to eat fresh eye-wateringly expensive lobster.

If she expressed interest in a play, he'd surprise her with front-row tickets. If she'd just read the book of the moment, Gerrard would have found where the author was holding events and somehow, with all his contacts and charm, get them both invites.

Theirs was a whirlwind romance. He literally worked his way into her life and before she knew it, she'd got to the point of imagining life without him as unthinkable. And she'd loved him, she truly had. He was amusing, well-informed and such a gentleman.

Things moved fast. Before she knew it they were engaged and although she was slightly uneasy at the speed with which his presence was changing her life, she believed his affections would cool down to a manageable level.

He'd soon find other things to focus on besides her, then he wouldn't be quite so obsessive in phoning and texting her constantly.

But when Gerrard, unbidden, went ahead and bought her a car, just like that, it seemed a bit too over the top — almost as if he was hoping to make her dependent upon him.

They'd talked about buying a house and had even browsed the net and been to see one or two. But then, without warning, Gerrard announced to her one evening that he'd visited the estate agent and put down a deposit on one of the houses. He'd gone and made a unilateral decision without her.

Siobhan had protested.

'We should have come to that decision together. We should have been equal partners.'

'We did, silly.' He'd pushed her concerns aside. 'Don't you remember, we saw a house on that same new estate and you said it was ideal, that you loved it, that it's exactly the sort of place you'd like to live.'

'But we hadn't jointly made a final decision, and even if we had, we should have gone to see the estate agent together. We're a couple after all.'

'What does it matter, Siobhan? The one I've offered on is exactly the same house as the one I saw with you, but in a different place on the development

— a better place, actually.

'It's south facing so it gets more sun. You'll love it. What's more, I managed to negotiate a reduction. Negotiations are always much easier when there are fewer people involved.'

She was miffed but he arranged an immediate viewing and it was a lovely house. It was the sort of house she'd have chosen, given half the chance.

Nevertheless, the experience planted a seed of doubt deep inside, which niggled at her making her wonder. She only started having serious concerns when Gerrard began talking incessantly about her not needing to work in the future.

'But I love my job, it's part of who I am. I'm too young to give it up and why should I want to?'

'Because it takes you away from me too much. You could start up your own little business or something, one you can run from home. I'll finance it, don't you worry. I love you, sweetheart, I want to be with you whenever I can. I know you're very bright and it gives you lots to think about but there are loads of ways you can get that intellectual stimulation.

'I can give you much of what you need there — we talk for hours, don't we? Why would you need other people when you've got me?'

It wasn't that at all. She'd always had lots of friends, though she had noticed them getting more distant the more Gerrard took over her every waking minute.

As is so often the way, it took a friend, a real friend, to make her begin to see the light. She and her girlfriend Annie had had a couple of glasses of prosecco at Siobhan's little London flat.

It was one of the few evenings Gerrard hadn't been able to monopolise her company because he'd had an important work do where partners weren't invited.

The subject of Gerrard had come up. Unlike Siobhan's other friends, Annie had never warmed to him.

'Are you sure marrying Gerrard is the right thing to do?'

'Why wouldn't it be?' Siobhan had challenged her. Everything had been arranged. Gerrard had spared no expense on the enormous wedding.

'I've been saving for this day for years, darling,' he'd assured her when her eyes widened at the cost of everything. The event had gained a momentum way above the modest affair Siobhan had originally planned.

'Because, Siobhan.' Annie had waved her glass at her, 'he's just soooo controlling. Can't you see what's happening? You're flattered by all the attention he's paying you and what woman wouldn't be, but it's getting to the point where he's calling all the shots.

'Your friends are complaining they never get to see you. We can't even get to talk to you on the phone.'

'He doesn't like me taking calls when we're out together.'

'But you're always out together. He's

monopolising you, can't you see, it's not healthy?'

Siobhan couldn't initially and she was very cool with Annie. But, as things moved inexorably closer to the wedding day Siobhan realised it wasn't so much that she was making plans with Gerrard but that he was making plans for her.

He was beginning to infantilise her, treat her like a child who couldn't make her own decisions.

'It's so good that you agreed to that house in the end. Living in Berkshire near my mother and father will be lovely for them and for you.

'When I'm away they can keep an eye on you, especially when we have children. You won't have any time for work. You can join the local book group and the tennis club and work on designing each room in the house. You could dabble in interior design. That's a job you could do from home. I'll look up courses for you.'

She gritted her teeth. Gerrard was planning her whole existence. Annie's words came crashing back and suddenly, Siobhan felt as if she were literally drowning under Gerrard's suffocating love.

It was then she'd made the brave decision to call the whole thing off. It had caused huge ructions, particularly with her mother.

Life for Caroline as a single mother hadn't been easy. Siobhan realised only too well that for her mother, security, and a husband who earned a good wage for her daughter was of utmost importance.

To ditch all that, to turn her back on it, to cancel all those expensive arrangements, to disappoint Gerrard who did, after all was said and done, love her to bits had been hard. It was a fairy tale gone sour for all involved, and Siobhan had felt so guilty.

He wasn't a bad man, just a misguided one. Maybe it would be good to meet Gerrard again, just to clear the air. After all, they had mutual friends and were bound to meet on occasion in London. For there to be any tension would be horrible.

Siobhan put her mobile phone back in the pocket of her skirt. Today she had worn a bright white and yellow spotted thirties-style shirt-waister dress with a matching scarf wrapped around her hair. Happy clothes because this morning she'd woken with the sun, she'd felt bright and breezy and had skipped downstairs.

Now she walked back towards the breakfast table and her feet dragged heavily across the stones of the patio.

'Everything OK?' Christian's eyes were hooded with concern.

He was moved to place a hand softly on her shoulder. The touch was reassuring, gentle, but she was surprised that no thrill ran down her arm as it had when their hands had brushed before. It was almost as if Gerrard were here already, keeping tabs on her. She felt tenseness rise in her throat, but gave Christian a reassuring smile.

'I'm absolutely fine. A friend,' she

didn't say ex-fiancé, 'of mine is in Thiviers, purely by chance. He's staying close by, and is popping around to La Refuge to see me today if that's OK.'

'Of course, it is absolutely fine. While you are here, this house is to be treated as your own. All your friends are welcome.'

'Thank you.' She didn't doubt that Christian would fling open the doors in his inimitable generous way. How could he possibly have any notion of how potentially uncomfortable Gerrard's presence might make things?

'I'm really sorry,' she added, 'but it means I'll have to put off you showing me around the porcelain works this afternoon.'

'No problem. The porcelain works will always be there. We can go tomorrow morning.'

'Thank you, Christian. And now, I have to go upstairs and do some research. Although a large proportion of objects here will be usable for the film, as they come from exactly the right period in history, some aren't.

'Part of my job is to ensure everything's authentic or else we'll be inundated with letters from people who've spotted something out of keeping historically. I'll be holed up with my books. Thank you for a wonderful breakfast.'

Siobhan needed to be alone. Christian gave her a lingering glance as she departed.

Peace is Shattered

Siobhan had only been upstairs an hour when she heard the crunching of a car on the gravel driveway, and a great commotion downstairs. The sound of a hooter blaring loudly, car doors banging one after another, a woman's voice, laughing, shrieking and a man's voice softer, more measured. More girlish voices which she recognised as Janique's and Mariette's joined the cacophony. What on earth was going on?

Siobhan made her way down to the front of the house and there saw a magnificent shiny racing green Mark II Jaguar. Christian was lugging suitcases from it, his muscular arms coping well with the weight as he grappled with what looked like enough luggage for 10 people.

There in front of him, barking orders

like an excited chihuahua, stood a young woman, with an angelic face. She wore a purple body-hugging dress which left nothing to the imagination.

Long, slender legs ended in five-inch-high heels as she struggled over the pebbles of the drive.

'Christian, sweetie — that's your name, isn't it? You'll have to get some sort of boarding laid here, I can't possibly keep going over these dreadful stones every time I come in or out. They'll ruin my Laboutins, they're worth a fortune.

'They didn't cost me, mind you. I was given them free just to be seen wearing them, but I need to keep them looking nice or they won't send me any more and I do love a fancy shoe, sweetie.'

This, Siobhan realised from having seen a fashion spread in a Sunday supplement with the headline 'Watch out, Hollywood, here comes your next bombshell', was Miss Philadelphia Grant. That face was entrancing, the personality perhaps less so.

Scurrying behind her, looking weary, was Roger Rivers, the director of the forthcoming film which was soon to be shot at La Refuge. Siobhan knew Roger well, and 'The Hallowe'en Haunting' was to be his next award-winning triumph.

Surprised was not the word for Siobhan's horror at having the peace of La Refuge interrupted a fortnight before filming was to begin.

These few heavenly days were supposed to be her golden time, her chance to get all the props perfectly in order, catalogued and listed for each scene.

An early arrival of any of the others involved was a disaster, particularly a starlet like Philadelphia. Siobhan had been around such girls before. They were endlessly demanding, like a whirlpool around which everything revolved.

But, ever the professional, Siobhan plastered on a welcoming smile and held out her hand in greeting. Philadelphia completely blanked her and was asking Christian at the top of her lungs for 'something to drink, I'm absolutely parched, as dry as a sheet of sandpaper, sweetie'.

'Hello, how lovely to see you, Roger,' Siobhan said, while behind her hand she hissed, 'a full two weeks early.'

They could chat quietly without Philadelphia hearing, as the young actress was laughing and giggling with Mariette who was completely awestruck at meeting a real life model. That very moment, she was oohing and aahing at the many jewelled bracelets, rings and necklaces which dripped, glistening in the sun, from Philadelphia's over gar-landed but undeniably impressive body.

Roger, sporting a round paunch from too many business lunches, and with a permanently lined forehead, neverthe-less looked jaunty in his linen jacket and ever-present bright bow tie.

This one was pink. He never travelled with fewer than seven in his suitcase, a different colour for every day of the week.

'I know, so sorry we've turned up early, Siobhan. Philadelphia's latest photo shoot was cancelled due to storms in the Caribbean. She was threatening to take off to Costa Rica to go and see an ex-boyfriend who's an extremely bad influence.

'She's so wilful I just know she'd have ended up partying like there was no tomorrow and then been late for the shoot. Nannying Philadelphia is a full time job but I have to protect my assets, don't I? It was better for me to bring her here — at least I know where she is and what she's up to.

'She's got lines to learn, too. The dreadful girl confessed to me on the plane she's barely looked at them. Believe me,' he wiped the sweat from his forehead, 'I'm an unwilling Mary Poppins. Isn't she gorgeous, though — until she opens her mouth, that is?'

'But what are we going to do with her?' Siobhan asked in despair. 'It'll be far too quiet for her here, she's a party animal. She's not going to sit 24 hours

106

a day studying lines.'

'I'll make sure she learns her lines if it kills me. I'm also planning to take her off to all the best restaurants and find people for her to meet. We can do some pre-filming publicity, she'll lap that up. I've already got 'Paris Match' and 'Le Monde' coming to visit.

'When we're not doing that, you'll think of something, Siobhan, I'm sure. Imagine you're her older, wiser sister.'

'Oh, no, I'm rubbish at babysitting, Roger.' But Siobhan's words fell on stony ground, Roger was already off, linking his arm around Philadelphia's minute waist and marching her round to the patio.

'Mariette,' Philadelphia called, 'how about a little drinkie?'

Siobhan stood on the driveway, lips pursed, watching the tiny entourage float off. Philadelphia's voice crooned to Christian in a flirty way.

'Thank heavens you're sorting the pool, I can't bear this heat. And how lovely, is that a boathouse with canoes?

Roger, you must find someone to take me out on the river canoeing, so romantic.'

Philadelphia took a long, unabashed look at Christian as she spoke, fluttering impossibly thick eyelashes. It seemed there wasn't a man alive she didn't want to flirt with and didn't mind who knew it.

'This place is darling, isn't it? I'm going to make the most of all the facilities while I'm here. In fact, I might stay for ever.'

Christian shot Siobhan a look as if to say he hoped he wasn't going to be mistaken for one of the facilities and Siobhan shot him a sympathetic look back. Then she made her way off to follow Philadelphia and be sociable.

Cocktails were what Philadelphia demanded, in every available variety. Mariette was only too happy to oblige. Philadelphia displayed herself like an exotic butterfly, laughing and joking and downing a pina colada, a strawberry daiquiri and an espresso martini, one after the other as if they were lemonade.

Full of cocktails and after burning brightly in the midday sun, Philadelphia, like the unruly kittens she'd spent ages playing with, giggling loudly at all their antics, suddenly declared she was shattered.

'Where's my bedroom?'

She was taken upstairs and Siobhan was relieved that they didn't see her for another three hours. Peace finally reigned.

* * *

A solid lunch was obviously something Philadelphia didn't have very often if her pencil-thin legs were anything to go by. She seemed to exist on the alcohol and cigarettes which she fished out of her expensive Birkin handbag. It probably cost as much as Siobhan made in a year.

Roger, on the other hand, happily indulged in duck pate, cheese, fresh walnuts, peaches and bread which Christian had hastily rustled up, like a magician, from somewhere.

A while later, Christian encountered Siobhan going upstairs.

'Are you OK? You look tired.'

'I was so enjoying the peace and quiet here, and now it's all been lost. I don't know how I shall do my own work if I have to help Roger entertain Philadelphia.'

'Don't worry,' Christian said kindly. 'The pool will be ready later today and Mariette for one will help keep your young actress amused. She used to look after children in the school holidays to earn a euro or two. I do not think this will be much different.'

Siobhan giggled. Philadelphia was so much like a child, but a stunningly beautiful one, and she knew it. The camera loved Philadelphia. This film, if it was a success, would make her fortune.

Siobhan wondered if that was part of the reason Roger had been able to get the girl here early. Someone as brazen and self-consciously confident as Philadelphia might be hiding insecurities which meant she'd wanted to be here early to settle in before the others arrived.

A film set could be a daunting place, especially if you were new to it.

'I have some work of my own to do upstairs but I'll be down later. Thank you so much for all your help.'

'And I am grateful for yours. You said you would help me solve the mystery of Marie-Louise and for that I am very happy.'

'Of course I will,' Siobhan said, 'though I'm not sure how much we'll see of our ghost now that La Refuge has been invaded.'

'We'll see.' Christian said. 'Philadelphia is very young and so was Marie-Louise. It may be that our ghost might respond to her youth. Young people often have paranormal sightings. Their energy seems to attract spirits.'

With that, he made his way off to check on progress at the swimming pool.

An Uncomfortable Reunion

By late afternoon, the pool was glistening, the pump had been mended and the crystal-clear water rippled seductively. Lavender scent hung like expensive perfume on the summer air.

Around the pool Christian had placed loungers and a large green umbrella. Under the trees next to the pool he had strung up hammocks in the shade. Late evening sunbeams, golden and still heating the air, sparkled on the water. Aquamarine tiles had been scrubbed clean and there could surely be nothing more inviting than the cool, refreshing water.

'Siobhan,' Philadelphia called as Siobhan wandered up to survey the pool's transformation, 'we haven't properly met.'

Philadelphia was lounging, hand

limply outstretched, sporting an impossibly large pair of sunglasses and an impossibly brief yellow bikini. The Raybans made her tiny, perfect face look even more like a young fawn's.

She lifted the sunglasses as Siobhan approached and the older girl could see why the young actress was such a sought after model. Her face was perfectly symmetrical. Framed by thick shapely brows and dark sultry false lashes, her eyes were captivating. Her lips were full and voluptuous.

Behind the bravado, Siobhan sensed a grain of loneliness. Could it be possible Philadelphia, with all her beauty and golden future ahead, might never know who to trust in the cut-throat world of entertainment?

'Lovely to meet you. Did you have a good sleep?'

'Yes, thanks, though it took me ages to drop off. Those birds make a terrific racket, don't they? And that constant rustling of leaves on the trees freaks me out. So does the buzzing. There are bees and bugs everywhere — they frighten me. Everything stings, doesn't it, in places like this?'

'I like that sound. I think it's soothing.' The girl's rejection of all the lovely things La Refuge had to offer rubbed Siobhan up the wrong way.

'It's proper countryside here, for miles and miles. A rare treat nowadays,' Siobhan said. She had a sneaking suspicion girls like Philadelphia would only ever be happy in somewhere as artificial as she was herself.

'It might be a treat to you but where is everybody? Why aren't there any houses nearby? It's nothing like New York or London, is it? There are no night clubs or pubs, no places to see and be seen. What on earth do people do all day in places like this? It would drive me crazy.'

Siobhan gave her a weak smile. Read books perhaps, she thought. Go for long, delicious country walks. Spend hours cooking wonderful food.

'No-one would see you from one day

to the next if you lived here. You could die and no-one would know it.' Philadelphia sat up in a chair and suddenly gave up her pout. 'The only interesting thing about this place is the ghost. Have you heard about the ghost?'

'I have,' Siobhan said, 'on the first day I was here, I even thought I saw it.'

'Wow!' Philadelphia's eyes rounded like saucers. 'Where?'

'At the window of the old porcelain works.'

'What did it look like, male or female?'

'A young girl. It was only a fleeting glance. There is a painting in the dining-room of a girl in a boat, it looks a lot like her. In fact, I'm not sure I saw anything really, the sun here's so bright, it plays tricks with the eyes. I don't really believe in ghosts.'

'Well, I do. What's more, I reckon that's the only good thing about this crumbling old pile. Why don't we set up cameras and stuff to record it, and microphones and things? I've seen it done on those TV programmes.

'I could get the techy guys to sort it when they get here. I can wrap them around my little finger.' Philadelphia wound one thickly gorgeous skein of hair around her finger. 'We'd be sure to catch your silly old ghost that way.'

Siobhan was appalled. No-one wanted to 'catch' the ghost of poor Marie-Louise. Christian would be horrified. The idea of seeking her out was only in order to find out what happened to her, to give her spirit some sort of closure, rather than turn her story into a circus.

'I think Roger would have something to say about that,' Siobhan said hastily. 'CCTV type cameras everywhere would show up in the scenes in the film.'

The whole notion was ridiculous. Philadelphia was obviously a girl who didn't think things through before she opened her mouth. Maturity, sadly, wasn't one of her many talents. But then, Siobhan reminded herself, she wasn't much more than a teenager, far from home and any parental guidance. She'd been swept up in the world of entertainment and there was precious little guidance there.

'Have you tried the pool yet?' Siobhan asked, desperate to get off the subject of Marie-Louise. With her butterfly mind, Philadelphia was easily distracted.

'No, I was just going in — you coming?'

As Philadelphia got up and her figure was revealed in all its glory, Siobhan could see one of the reasons she was so popular and her Instagram account had millions of followers. She was any photographers' dream.

At the pool, Siobhan dived in quickly. She'd never be as stunningly attractive as Philadelphia. She smiled wryly underwater, acknowledging that she would always be a behind the scenes girl rather than centre stage. But she didn't mind; she loved her job and that she could go about her business and not be mobbed at airports or out shopping. Philadelphia must lead an odd life.

Siobhan bubbled up to the surface, delighting in the cool fresh water washing over her skin and rippling through her hair.

She noticed though that Philadelphia was making her way gingerly into the water not wanting to spoil her carefully groomed locks. The poor girl was so obsessive about her looks. Everything had to remain perfect. What did it matter if her hair got messed up here in the middle of nowhere? Philadelphia seemed to live, eat and breathe the persona she'd cultivated. Siobhan wondered what the real girl was like underneath.

Philadelphia swam around sedately, occasionally splashing and obviously enjoying the water when suddenly, she stopped, her gaze fixed in the distance.

Coming through the trees was a tall, smart-suited figure with sandy coloured hair and a confident gait. Siobhan recognised him instantly. Gerrard had arrived. Her heart lurched. Whether it was through misplaced desire, for she had desired him very much once, or from apprehension about what their meeting was going to bring, Siobhan didn't know.

She wished she wasn't half dressed and in a swimming pool. Suddenly, she felt very inadequate. On the other hand, Philadelphia had taken a long cool look as she did with every man, like a cat sizing up a mouse. She swam over to the pool steps and made her way out, slowly, deliberately, knowing she commanded centre stage.

Gerrard was transfixed.

'Hello.' The young girl's voice was soft and suggestive. 'Who are you?' She tossed back a wayward skein of hair and stood hands on hips.

'My name's Gerrard,' he said, beads of sweat appearing on his forehead. 'That water looks good. Don't I recognise you from somewhere?'

'You should.' Her laugh tinkled like

chiming bells. 'If my publicist has been doing his work properly. I'm Philadelphia Grant.' She extended her hand. 'You should come and have a dip, shouldn't he, Siobhan?'

Gerrard finally noticed his former fiancée.

'Oh, hi, Siobhan. Sorry, sorry, I didn't see you there, the sun was in my eyes. I didn't want to come at dinner time, I thought that might be inconvenient, so I came now. I don't want to interrupt you ladies.'

'You two know each other?' Philadelphia looked intrigued.

'Er, yes. Gerrard is a . . . an old friend from London.'

'You don't look like a film person,' Philadelphia said, probing. 'You look more like a banker, an entrepreneur, maybe a property developer.' She was fishing, flirting, and Siobhan got the distinct impression, trying to work out the number of noughts which might appear at the end of Gerrard's impressive bank balance.

'A bit of all of those, actually.'

At that moment, Christian arrived with a welcome jug of fresh lemonade, chinking with ice cubes and topped with borage and mint. The aroma was intoxicating, the scent of summer in a glass. It was a welcome interruption and Siobhan wondered if Christian, who knew the goings-on in the house almost as if by osmosis, had deliberately turned up at that point. It certainly made the situation less awkward for her.

Siobhan climbed up the steps of the pool and wrapped herself in her towelling robe. Standing by Philadelphia, Siobhan felt like a dowdy sparrow beside an extravagant bird of paradise.

She clutched her dripping hair and twisted it round her hand. Siobhan was suddenly ashamed of it, and of her retro style. The white Thirties-inspired swimming costume she wore, with its halter neck and bow, covered up more than it revealed. It made her feel dowdy in a way it never had before.

'Nice to meet you.' Christian shook Gerrard's hand. 'Please take a seat. Can I offer you some refreshment?'

He poured lemonade and handed the glasses round as they sat at the table, the sound of the pool gently bubbling in the background.

Considering everything else Christian had to do, she was grateful to him for looking after them all so well. Running along behind him with serviettes, bonbon dishes of salted cashews and homemade cheese biscuits and a bottle, was Mariette.

'I zink zat you might want some of this, too.' She almost winked as she waved the bottle of gin in Philadelphia's direction. Christian directed a frown towards Mariette. The alcohol obviously wasn't his idea. But before he had the chance to get Mariette to take it back inside, Philadelphia had grabbed it and slopped a liberal slug into her glass.

'You look like a gin drinker to me, Gerrard.' Without waiting for an answer, she'd topped his glass up with a double measure.

'Well, yes, I am pretty keen on craft gins, and it is the cocktail hour, isn't it?' The two of them clinked their glasses and drank. It was clear that Mariette wanted to model herself on Philadelphia. Siobhan noticed the youngster who normally only wore a dash of mascara and clear lipgloss was fully made up with smoky black eyes and bright orange lipstick as if she was going to a party.

'I shouldn't really be seen drinking Red Sparrow gin,' Philadelphia said. 'I'm just about to earn a shedload of money endorsing Harrison's gin and it's in my contract that I shouldn't be seen in public drinking anyone else's. I won't tell, though, if you don't.'

They chatted, drank all the lemonade, and ate all the nuts. Mariette hung on Philadelphia's every word and Siobhan despaired of being able to have a private chat with Gerrard.

Philadelphia had obviously taken to him. She sat with her hand on her chin as she asked him endless questions, listening to the replies in between regaling them with her tales of the modelling world.

Siobhan had to hand it to Philadelphia, she was amusing and fun, and Siobhan could see why men fell at her feet. Gerrard and she were getting on like a house on fire.

Christian sat and drank his lemonade quietly, interjecting as necessary when they asked questions about the house. Every now and then, Siobhan caught him looking at her, as if he were making sure she was all right.

The time ran on and it was 7 p.m. Roger emerged from the house.

'Sorry I've left you all on your own, but I had to make some phone calls. Our chief lighting man's managed to get himself a dose of pneumonia and there are doubts he'll be ready in time for the shoot. We have had to ring round and find out if anyone else might be available. It's a nightmare. Anyhow, I could do with some dinner.

'Philadelphia, you and I have been invited out with a contact not far from here. He's an investor, he's a useful guy to know and I want to interest him in our next project. He's sending a car for us — it'll be here in half an hour.'

'Then I'd better get ready.' Philadelphia shot up and was gone, leaving everyone else to clear up.

Gerrard looked at his watch.

'Good heavens, is that the time? I had no idea I'd been here this long, and I have a conference call I have to make back at my hotel. I'm so sorry, Siobhan, I really didn't see how the time was going, it's just rushed by. Can I call again tomorrow afternoon?'

Siobhan felt like a deflated ballon. She'd wound herself up, expecting a serious chat with Gerrard and to lay old differences to rest. But Philadelphia had monopolised the proceedings and the evening hadn't panned out as she'd expected.

'Yes, of course, that's fine,' she said, though she didn't relish having a night and a morning to churn everything over in her head again.

'I'll put the chairs straight, and sweep up the crumbs,' she said to Christian when the others had gone back into the house. She knew how important it was to clear food as Christian had told her that there were wild boars around who dug up holes in the lawn if they were encouraged near the house.

'You don't need to, I can do it,' he said.

'No, I want to. I really appreciate you welcoming Gerrard like you did and waiting hand and foot on Philadelphia. She's a handful.'

'No worries,' Christian said, 'as long as you're OK,' and went off to wash the glasses.

The pool area seemed so quiet now they had all gone. It was twilight, and an owl hooted in the tree canopy, its voice calling eerily through the trees. The heat of the day had dropped dramatically and the light was failing as Siobhan brushed the table and chairs.

Siobhan suddenly had the sense of not being alone. She stopped her brushing and listened. A breeze had arisen and as she stood silently, she could have sworn she heard a long pained sigh. The sound sent shivers up her spine and yet, and yet . . .

A Trick of the Light?

Siobhan strained her ears to listen more closely. Was it just the sound of the breeze in the trees, the rustle of the wind through the leaves? It had been so noisy when they'd all been laughing and chatting round the table, and now in the margins between day and night, it was as if the house and gardens were claiming their place again in her consciousness.

She heard footfall behind her, turned swiftly and there, standing in the shadows was a barefooted Philadelphia.

'Sorry!' Philadelphia exclaimed. 'Sorry, Siobhan, I didn't mean to sneak up on you. I think I left my sunglasses down here — they cost a fortune. I don't want to lose them. There they are, tucked in the cushion of the sun bed. Isn't this a beautiful time of day?'

'It is,' Siobhan agreed.

'Do you think there are many animals here? I like animals but I can't have any pets because I'm always away somewhere. It wouldn't be fair on them. But I'd so love a dog or a cat.'

Philadelphia, on her own, one to one, was quite a different prospect from Philadelphia with an audience. She seemed less self-conscious, less needing to make an impression.

'There are all sorts of animals here, squirrels and tiny mice who rustle through the undergrowth. The kittens are always being spooked by them.'

'The idea of the ghost spooks me,' Philadelphia said. 'I . . . I thought I heard something just now, when I was walking down here, like someone sighing.' So, Philadelphia had heard it too. 'It came from the trees over there, in the direction of that old building.'

'The porcelain works,' Siobhan said. The two of them stood in silence. The light was really fading now, the cornflower blue sky had turned sapphire, then aquamarine and was now a stark navy blue with the first star appearing. The two girls peered in the half light, their night vision developing. Suddenly, Siobhan felt Philadelphia's long nails digging into her arm.

'Oh, my goodness, look over there.'

'What?' Siobhan hissed.

'There's something moving, I swear it.'

As Siobhan looked, she couldn't make out anything clearly. The poplar leaves had silver backs and in the half light, they caught the corner of the eye. If one had an over-active imagination, they could easily be mistaken for someone wandering through the trees.

'It's a skirt, someone's standing there in a long skirt, a long white skirt. It's the ghost,' Philadelphia hissed, 'I swear it.'

Siobhan was going to tell her she was imagining it but then, when she peered more closely, she saw a glimpse, just a flash, of something which did indeed look like the long skirt of a woman. It was so dark now, her eyes were straining. She felt her blood surge, and her heart quicken.

'Come on,' Philadelphia said, 'let's go and have a look. Let's flush her out.'

'No,' Siobhan said. If it was the ghost of Marie-Louise, she didn't want to scare her away. If they could see her, the spirit might be able to see them as she wandered, troubled, through the grounds.

'I'm not scared.' Philadelphia shot off in her bare feet into the trees. Siobhan couldn't let her go on her own so she ran to catch her up. Then, there came a resounding, 'Ouch, that hurt.'

'What is it?' Siobhan could barely see Philadelphia through the thick undergrowth.

'I've stood on a pine cone,' Philadelphia hopped up and down, making the most fearful noise. If there had been a ghost anywhere near, she would have frightened it off for certain.

As Philadelphia was rubbing her foot, Siobhan leant down to see if any proper damage had been done. It was too dark.

In the quiet though, Siobhan became conscious of something flapping, waving in the breeze on one of the bushes, low down near the ground. She bent and untangled it from the thorns of a wild rose.

'I think this might be our ghost,' she said, and held up in her hand, a white tea towel.

'What's it doing here?'

'It's one of Christian's special linen tea towels. I understand what happened now. The washing line is close to here and as the evening breeze has blown up, the tea towel's obviously come off its pegs and ended up caught on this bush. There, that's our ghost.'

Philadelphia held the piece of cloth in her hands and looked at Siobhan.

'Well, it's possible, I suppose, but I know that's not what I saw. I saw thinner fabric than that, more like muslin, and more of it. What's more, it was hanging straight, not blowing about.'

As they made their way back to the

house, Siobhan wondered if she was right, though quite frankly she didn't know what to think. Perhaps their eyes had been playing tricks on them, perhaps not. Philadelphia had had quarter of a bottle of gin — she wasn't exactly a reliable witness.

All Siobhan knew as she finally lay in bed that night, was that she needed her sleep. But her dreams were many and unsettled. Over and over again, she saw trees, a dark summer's night and a girl in a long skirt walking in the woods by the riverside. Then a girl floating down the river in a boat, her eyes closed, her fair hair swirling as if she were under the water, not on it, and her body was lifeless floating down, down, down. Around her, jewels swirled. Siobhan could distinctly see a gold necklace hung with three charms, faith, hope and charity, a ruby ring, a string of pearls.

When Siobhan awoke, the images of the young girl were etched in her psyche just as surely as if she had seen them in real life, and not in a dream.

When she finally crawled out from the covers after a restless night, she went to the window and looked out over the garden.

Dawn was just breaking. As Siobhan watched the sun peek over the trees, she saw a figure moving around down by the boathouse. Strong limbs, wide capable shoulders. Christian was doing his morning rounds. She suddenly had a yen to be with him and to explore, and this would be the best time to do it, this golden hour before the rest of the house awoke.

Quickly, she pulled on a pair of loose jeans and a roomy shirt, ideal for messing about in boats. She fastened a green scarf round her hair and slipped on a pair of canvas loafers and she was off. Christian looked overjoyed to see her as her feet crunched over the gravel.

'You're up early.'

'I know, out and about before breakfast. The thing is, it got a bit crowded round here yesterday and I missed our proposed visit to the porcelain works. I know it's early, but could we do it now? And could we make our way down there by boat, would that be possible?'

He beamed her that special smile.

'Indeed it would. I'd be happy to take you.' He gathered the coil of rope he was handling and fixed it fast and neat.

'The river is, of course, the route that Pierre Seydoux's grandfather, Gaston Seydoux was used to taking. He liked to check regularly on the flow of the river, to make sure it was moving well. Water was not only needed in the production process but the river was essential for deliveries.

'There are records, after storms, of large trees falling upriver and disrupting the flow. When that happened, Gaston Seydoux would get together a large work party to drag the tree out of the river and restore the flow. Although many of the materials arrived here on the road by horse and cart, many came by boat.

'In a busy little factory there was a

constant process of products in, such as all the raw materials, the kaolin and cobalt oxide for the glaze, and wood to heat the ovens and the kilns. But also they needed to get products out.

'All that fine china, the vases, plates, cups and saucers would begin their journey to the fine houses and royal families of the rest of Europe and the world from this isolated place.

'By using the river regularly, Gaston would be able to check the levels and make sure all was well.' So saying, Christian entered the boathouse and untied one of the canoes.

'In Gaston's day, he would use a wooden rowing boat, not a fibreglass canoe.' He dragged the canoe to the water's edge.

'Now, there is a technique to getting in. You get in the front and sit quite still. I will get in the back and push us off from the banks of the river with my paddle. Do not think though that you are going to get away scot free without doing any of the work.'

'So you've got a paddle for me, too? And here was I thinking I could just lounge.'

'No lounging for you, young lady. Here you go.'

They paddled down the river and it wasn't half as easy as it looked.

'The current here is unpredictable. Can you see the water swirling? There are dips and troughs. Gaston would have known every tiny whirlpool and gully.'

The river, with steam rising upwards, was magical this early in the morning. They paddled underneath aged overhanging willows which dipped their fingers into the water.

'There's a kingfisher,' Siobhan declared, 'I've never seen one before.'

'Yes, we are blessed here with those striking birds.'

'You said, Christian, that when Marie-Louise disappeared, this river was thoroughly searched.'

'It was. It was assumed that Marie-Louise had drowned. At one point, the mayor even demanded that the river be dammed to help the search and make it shallower, as at points it is very deep. Gaston complained bitterly. Rich, mean and ruthless, he was a very unpopular man amongst the townspeople.

'Even though the river was dammed as the mayor had ordered, it stormed that day, and the rain was so torrential that it washed mud from the river banks on to the river floor. The banks would ironically normally have been protected by the height of the river, but they were exposed. This meant that quantities of mud were washed that day on to the exposed riverbed.

'Ironically, the damming of the river may have made the chances of finding any corpse that might have been disposed of, less likely.

'Marie-Louise's body was never found. Shortly after, Gaston ordered a new storage wing to be built on the side of the porcelain works. There were rumours that he may have had her body buried underneath the foundations but of course by this time all manner of crazy rumours abounded.

'Poor Marie-Louise had turned from a simple village girl into a myth, a legend which kept on being embellished so that the truth became mired through the years in hearsay, gossip and fanciful stories. I know this better than most, Marie-Louise being my distant relative.

'I heard so many stories in my youth even my mother has said she doesn't know what is real and what is not. She carries a locket around her neck enclosing a superb miniature painting Marie-Louise executed of herself.

'It is a stunning self-portrait painted on a tiny disc of porcelain and is one of my mother's prized possessions. She never takes it off. It is she, as much as myself, who is desperate to know the truth.

'She said to me only the other day, 'Christian, I have less of my life in front of me than I have behind me. Before I die I want to know the truth. I despair of ever knowing what happened to our poor relative. I feel not knowing the truth is a stain on our family'.'

As they paddled through the water, negotiating the still parts of the river where it was shallowest, and the deeper parts where the water swirled and eddied alarmingly, Siobhan felt herself lucky to be in the hands of such an expert canoeist.

They reached the porcelain works and docked their canoe by the main building where Christian tied it to a waiting pole at the jetty. Siobhan looked back at La Refuge, nestling behind the trees.

From where they stood, she could see its roof and chimneys and could follow the path of the river, right to the house. She looked up at the porcelain works and the thing which most caught her attention was the window where on her first morning here, she had seen the face of a girl. It might have been a ghost, or it might have been a trick of the light.

'Can we go up there?' she asked.

'Of course. Anywhere you wish.'

Christian took a set of keys out of his pocket. They were old huge iron keys on a ring. None of the porcelain works had been modernised, all its doors and windows, everything about it was carefully preserved. In England, the building would have been taken up by a local history society and listed.

The main double doors at the back of the little factory, facing the river, were like heavy barn doors. There was an echo as Christian turned the lock and led her into a high ceilinged area.

'Clay reserves would have been brought here by rowing boat, nothing larger, as the river is too narrow at points to take bigger vessels. The clay would then be stored here on the ground floor.

'Also on this floor were general storerooms for all the raw materials, and as you can see, all the books of techniques and records of who had ordered what. They are all still here, on these shelves.'

One wall of the works was covered in ledgers, boxes containing old papers and heavy tomes describing various processes and techniques.

'They look like dry old technical books. Have you ever gone through them?'

'No,' Christian said. 'I don't think anybody has. The owner was once approached by a local historian who wanted to write a history of the porcelain works but in the end, he decided there was simply too much information to go through on his own.

'He decided better of it. I would love to have the time, but I've never found a spare minute. I was hoping at one time that Mariette or Janique might be interested but they are not.

'Be careful on the stairs, they're very steep, and hold the banister as you go up.'

'Wow!' Siobhan exclaimed as they got to the first floor. 'This place is fascinating! It looks as if the workers downed tools only yesterday. Everything's still here.'

In front of them was the workshop of the engravers, sculptors, plasterers and moulders. In the centre of the room stood a huge oven.

'Packing and repairs were also done on this floor and the packed articles would be roped down from these upper doors. See this hook?

'Pallets with the goods on would be carefully winched out of this room either through this door at the back and straight on to boats to go upriver, or out of the front on to carts drawn by horses to travel by road. Hundreds and thousands of beautiful highly gilded and carefully painted cups, saucers, jugs and plates would have been produced here in its heyday.'

They then made their way up the creaking wooden stairs to the loft.

'This is where Marie-Louise and the other painters, gilders and makers of animals and figures would have worked. They were a small, select and highly skilled team.'

Immediately, Siobhan was drawn to

the window. It was mired in cobwebs but she could clearly see out, over the treetops and towards La Refuge. This was the window, she realised, where the face had appeared to her on her first day here.

It might have been a trick of the light, the sun now fully up, was shining straight in, but it also might have been a real ghost. The more she soaked up the atmosphere in this room, the more she was convinced that Marie-Louise's ghost had looked out at her that day.

'This room,' Christian said, 'with its skylights, and facing south is deliberately placed to give the most light so that the painters and gilders could do their delicate work for as many hours in the day as possible.'

From this window, there was a direct eyeline across to La Refuge and it was high enough to see all the top rooms.

'From here, I can clearly see my room, where I'm sleeping. It was Gaston who slept there, wasn't it?'

'Yes, you are in the master bedroom,' Christian said.

'That's interesting,' she mused, and cogs and wheels started to turn in her head as she tried to work things out. Siobhan immediately realised that this was a perfect vantage point.

'From here, Marie-Louise and Gaston could have seen each other and known about each other's movements even in a time when there weren't mobile phones or any other phones, come to that.

'If Gaston and the young girl had had some sort of process of signalling each other, if they wanted to arrange secret trysts, it would be easy to do from here.'

There were two old wooden chairs and she and Christian sat down in them as they talked. Siobhan noticed that Christian brought his closer to her, as if to make her feel safe in this deserted, spooky space.

He was so close, he could have reached out and held her hand. She detected the tang of his aftershave on the air, sandalwood and eucalyptus, and the waft of newly shampooed hair. She breathed in deeply, enjoying his closeness.

'Last night, I had a strange dream.'

Siobhan related to Christian the things that had played out like a disjointed film during her troubled night's sleep.

'The answers are all here, in this building and in La Refuge, I'm sure of that. What's more, I'm even more sure having gone down the river with you that Marie-Louise's remains may still be somewhere in that water, even though her bones have never come to the surface, nor any clothing or other evidence.'

Christian looked troubled.

'But I cannot understand why her body would not have been found at some point over the years. The banks of this river have been strengthened and shored up as there has been erosion which, if it continued, might have threatened the foundations of La Refuge. If she had been buried somewhere along the banks she would have been found.

'I do not know what to think. For years I have gone over the possibilities in my head. For a while, I went through the transcripts of the search trying to find clues.

'Most of all, I wanted to know if she was done away with, and why someone should do that to someone so young and innocent. But then I became busy with other things. I feel I failed Marie-Louise by not continuing my search.'

'Then let me.' Siobhan jumped up.

'Let you what?'

'Continue the search. Work on the papers and books and documents here.'

'But that would be imposing on you and you have enough to do already.'

'I really made inroads into my work yesterday, despite having Philadelphia around. It's a good thing she naps so much and besides, I'm not her keeper.

147

She is, after all, an adult.'

'Not that she behaves like one.' It was one of the few barbed remarks she'd heard him make, it simply wasn't in his nature to be unkind.

But Siobhan sensed Christian was concerned that Philadelphia was too much of a party animal to be safe in the house. When the other film people arrived, anyone who didn't respect the precious objects in the house might endanger them. Christian, as guardian of the house, was rightly concerned to keep everything safe.

'I think Philadelphia's a bit lost, to be honest. She's very young and I've not heard her once mention her parents or family.

'She's in a world populated by sharks — the modelling and film worlds can be cruel, loving someone one minute and discarding them the next.'

'Maybe,' he said. 'I will try and be tolerant towards her.

'Well, if you really want to study the papers and books, feel free. There are also some boxes on the ground floor that haven't been opened by anyone to the best of my knowledge.'

'Then I shall start after breakfast. Speaking of which,' Siobhan's tummy rumbled, 'I'm ready for it now.'

They both stood up and as they did so, took one last look out of the window towards La Refuge.

'Oh, my word.' Siobhan clapped a hand over her mouth. 'Look, look up at my bedroom window, Christian. Do you see what I see?'

Siobhan felt her heart in her mouth. The sun had not reached the windows of the big house yet, this vision was no trick of the light.

So Close and Yet...

'Yes,' he said, his voice low and quiet, 'yes, yes, I see her, at your window.'

'Marie-Louise.' Siobhan gasped. 'A blonde-haired girl, her ghost. Oh no, her head's bent, as if in sorrow, I can't see her face. But I'm not imagining it, am I?'

'No, I see her, too. I have seen her here, many times, at this window, but never in Gaston's room.'

'Oh, Christian, do you understand what this means? That we are getting closer, you and I. That we will solve the mystery of Marie-Louise Thizy and how and why she died . . . and at whose hands.'

As they stood, eyes transfixed on the figure at the window, they suddenly heard an eerie sound. A bell chimed. One clear, sharp clang above their heads.

'What was that?'

Christian's brows knitted.

'The bell in the clock tower at the top of the factory works. It called workers in the morning. But it needs someone to pull the rope, it doesn't ring on its own.'

He ran at top speed across the attic room, down the rickety wooden stairs. Siobhan found him in the central courtyard, staring at a long rope which swung from side to side. There was no-one else to be seen.

'That frightened me,' Siobhan said, getting her breath back. 'Do you think it was the ghost who rang the bell?'

'I can think of no other explanation,' Christian said. 'This has never happened before. The bell rope is usually tethered.

'Even I am now scared. It almost feels as if our ghost is getting angry. I am not happy about you working here on your own, Siobhan.'

'I'm not scared of Marie-Louise. I'll be fine.'

'Nevertheless,' Christian said, 'please wait before you start looking at the books and papers here while I sort something out to help you to be less alone in your task.

'I wish I could help you myself but I have many things your director, Roger Rivers, has asked for. Come, let's have some breakfast and then I'll get things sorted.'

When they reached La Refuge, he went off to make a number of phone calls.

* ★ ★

At breakfast, Philadelphia stretched and yawned as if she'd had a long and heavy night's sleep.

'I think I'll just take it easy by the pool this morning. When did your friend Gerrard say he'd be back, Siobhan? I liked him. Besides, I'm bored.'

'I . . . I'm not sure.' Siobhan now felt very uneasy about seeing Gerrard again. The thought of their impending heart to heart was not something she was looking forward to.

Gerrard could be very controlling. She knew she'd have to be strong to assert herself, to confirm that they were finished. Fighting against a man who bordered on being a bully was exhausting.

Siobhan had noted Philadelphia's comment that she liked Gerrard. She wasn't sure if Philadelphia was playing games but she suspected that was just the sort of thing the girl was used to, and good at.

It was when Siobhan was helping Christian get the breakfast things washed that he turned to her.

'I have organised two things to help keep you company while you study the papers at the old porcelain works. One is Janique. She is very happy to help you as she is tired of cleaning at the house.

'Mariette, unfortunately, is desperate to spend more time with Philadelphia and has resolved to laze around the pool with her today. That girl is a bad influence on Mariette. My sister needs no encouragement to push against me. As an older brother, I have little influence now that the girls are both adults. I can see Philadelphia isn't good for Mariette but all I can do is keep a watching eye on my sister and try and make sure she isn't led astray. Any sort of danger being visited on her children has terrified my poor mother ever since my father died.'

'I'm sorry we've made your life difficult, Christian, when you already have enough to do.'

'Do not worry,' he said. 'My mother pronounced me head of the family when my father died but she said at the time it would not be easy, particularly with Mariette. She is a good girl, just impressionable.

'Now, as well as Janique coming to keep you company, there's this fella, too.'

So saying, Christian went out of the

back door and came back with the most gorgeous white Alsatian on a lead.

'Where on earth did you find him?'

'He belongs to one of my friends in Thiviers, an American guy called Nick Armstrong. The dog's name is Louis. Nick has a big sense of humour. It makes him laugh every time, particularly as the dog's a big fan of jazz music. Louis loves being with people.

'My friend is a construction engineer working on a big job at the airport at present and is unhappy that Louis is spending so much time on his own. He chews slippers and shoes if he gets bored.

'So Nick is only too happy for the dog to come here, as long as you can take Louis for a little walk every now and then.'

Siobhan knelt down and the dog wagged his tail so hard it banged on the floor. When Siobhan went to hug him, the dog came up to meet her and placed his paws on her shoulders, licking her neck.

'He's gorgeous. I won't feel scared or jittery no matter which ghosts visit. Who could be frightened with this lovely fellow to keep them company?'

'Good, that is agreed then. I must leave you now. Janique is in her room, so just let her know you are ready and she will accompany you to the porcelain works.'

'You're very kind, Christian.' Instinctively, Siobhan reached out to touch Christian on the arm, a gesture of friendship and appreciation for his care of her. His arm was warm and firm through the thin fabric of his cotton T-shirt. She liked the feeling of strength, and the way the muscles in his arm reminded her of statues of gods she had seen.

But Christian was real. Human, and all male, not at all like a cold marble statue. As she held him briefly, she could not deny that it wasn't just his friendship she appreciated, but his gorgeous smile, his wild hair, his closely shaven jaw.

She swallowed hard and felt her breath quickening. The attraction between them was undeniable and she realised it was mutual. Christian's hand came up and covered hers. Then, in a purely Gallic gesture, he brought her hand to his lips and kissed it. It was such a sweet gesture, so caressing, so intimate, so romantic.

Siobhan could feel the colour rushing to her face. She wanted more. His touch was gentle, captivating like an intoxicating liqueur. She moved her hand to his chin, to his cheek, and felt him move his face toward hers. He was so close now, he opened his lips as he brought them closer to hers. She could smell the scent of coffee on them, mixed with the glorious heady sandal-wood of his French aftershave.

A clock in the corner ticked, echoing the heartbeat ringing in her ears. So fast was her heart pounding she became dizzy as he brought his lips only a petal's depth away from hers. She wanted this so much, she hadn't realised quite how much until this delicious, heady, divine moment of madness.

Then, just as quickly as it had begun, the moment dissolved, like a bubble bursting on the air. Christian hastily let her go and took a pace backwards.

'I am sorry, I am very sorry.' His tone was clipped and embarrassed.

'Don't be!' she exclaimed. What had happened to change his mind? What had she done to turn him away? Hadn't she made her own feelings clear?

'I apologise I have acted badly.'

'Not at all. What do you mean?'

'Your 'friend' . . . ' Christian emphasised the word, filled it with meaning, loaded it with consequence.

'Gerrard, you mean?'

'Yes, Gerrard. I spoke to him yesterday before he left for the evening. He explained to me what your relationship is. That you were engaged, to be married.'

'Yes, we were . . . '

Christian was no longer looking at

her, his eyes resolutely on the ground.

'You don't have to explain. I have been remiss. The two of you, well, he said that the split was a foolish thing, over nothing and that he was here to effect a reconciliation. He said you are getting back together. I knew that and yet just now I acted badly.'

'But . . . ' Siobhan wanted to put her side, it wasn't like that at all. Gerrard had given Christian entirely the wrong impression.

Christian backed further away, his hands balled into fists.

'I know that is what his mission is and I do not want to spoil your chance of happiness. He is good looking, he is wealthy and successful, he will make a perfect husband for you . . . '

'It isn't like that, Christian . . . '

'I must go now. I am sorry, forgive me.' And with that, he was gone.

'Oh, Louis.' Siobhan knelt on the floor and took the warm, furry, comforting head of the dog in her hands. She nuzzled herself into his coat.

This was all so difficult and so embarrassing.

Christian clearly didn't have a lot of experience with women. Playing games wasn't in his nature. He was straight and honest. Unlike Gerrard, she thought, seething. Gerrard would do anything to get what he wanted.

She was livid. How dare he give Christian the impression that they were just about to take up again where they'd left off?

Siobhan had made it one hundred percent plain to him when she'd broken off their engagement that they would never get back together.

She stormed out of the kitchen and started to climb the stairs, Louis padding faithfully behind her. His warm nuzzle snuggled against her leg as if he could sense there was something amiss.

Her mind whirling, Siobhan realised in a moment of clarity that it was highly unlikely Gerrard had had any work near here. He'd never mentioned his company having any business in France.

He'd followed her here.

In his usual heavy-handed way, he'd pursued her and would try to get her back in his clutches by any means, fair or foul. He just couldn't resist trying to overpower people. Siobhan stomped up the stairs to the top floor.

Look how he'd been with Philadelphia yesterday. All women to him were like a conquest, he went through life notching them up on his personal score sheet. Siobhan was spitting mad. Gerrard was toxic.

She strode along the passage, the dog's claws still padding behind her on the wooden staircase before she realised she had gone up too many flights of stairs. She was at the very top of the house now. She was out of breath she'd walked so fast, but at least the exercise was calming her down a little.

Where on earth was she? She hadn't explored this far up. As she slowed down, she noticed a door ajar and in the room, which was bathed in sunlight, she saw a wall painting, a mural of a countryside scene.

'Louis,' she said as she pushed the door open more and went inside to see the mural more closely. 'This is the wall painting Christian mentioned. Look.'

Louis padded over and came to sit beside her. As she stroked him, a little tuft of snowy white fur careered up and wafted down again on the stifling summer air.

'There's Marie-Louise, isn't she beautiful? And see, oh my word, around her neck is the chain with the turquoise charms, the one I saw in my dreams.

'Marie-Louise is trying to speak to me from her grave. There's no other way I could have known about her necklace.' She could just make them out.

'They represent faith, hope and charity. Poor girl, she couldn't stand up for herself, so we must do it for her.'

'Well said.'

Siobhan whirled around to see Philadelphia standing at the door behind her. Siobhan had been so engrossed she'd not noticed the other girl.

'Is that poor Marie-Louise Thizy?'

'Yes, it is.'

'The ghost we saw last night.'

'If it was a ghost,' Siobhan said, 'it could just have been that washing on the line.'

Philadelphia ran her hand slowly over the wall painting.

'I think you want there to be a ghost, Siobhan.'

'What do you mean?'

'I think you're very practical, look at the job you do. Keeping everything in order, making sure all the objects in films are in keeping with the period. But at heart you're a romantic, you want there to be a mystery and you want to solve it.

'You're just like all the people who come to watch our films. They want a good story and they want it to end well.'

'There's not much wrong with that,

is there? It's making you and I a good living. We can all have our dreams and our audiences can have their happy ending.'

'That's true,' Philadelphia said. 'And despite what you might think about me, I'm not totally selfish, I want to make people happy.' She sighed, a resigned sound as if though only young, she could have sparks of wisdom.

'I come from a broken family. My father was on drugs a lot of the time and my mother took a long while to realise he wasn't going to change. She was so busy trying to make life better for him, I got sort of sidelined.

'He was always coming and going, making up, making my mum feel he was going to stay then flitting off. I had to rely a lot on my own imagination. I used to make up stories. I guess that's why I'm drawn to acting.

'I've always found modelling boring. Spending hours sitting around was a bit too much like the times I was a kid, left to my own devices. I'm a loner, I don't really fit in anywhere. Perhaps I never will.'

Siobhan studied Philadelphia and found sadness behind her eyes.

'This is a pretty painting.' Philadelphia changed the subject, as if she'd revealed too much of herself. 'And Marie-Louise is gorgeous, very natural looking. You couldn't get away with that now.

'You have to work hard to be considered beautiful these days. False nails, false eyelashes, hair extensions, it's exhausting being me. I wish I was you, you're naturally beautiful.'

'That's very kind but I know I'm plain.'

Philadelphia let out a laugh, a genuine, full throated laugh, not the sort of cynical false laughter Siobhan had heard yesterday, when Philadelphia was being the life and soul of the party because that's what she felt was expected of her.

'You're not plain at all, you're a classic beauty. Timeless.'

Siobhan, for the first time, felt sorry for the girl. Philadelphia had previously presented a self-confident, but very artificial young woman. Here, in the morning sunlight and devoid of makeup it was as if the real Philadelphia had been revealed.

If she was more often like this, Siobhan thought, she could have been truly likeable.

'And who's this, then?' Philadelphia patted the dog's head.

'His name's Louis. He belongs to a friend of Christian's.'

'I so want a dog. Something to love.'

'Why don't you get one?'

'I travel too often and for too long. It wouldn't be fair. Perhaps I could borrow him while I'm here. Take him for the odd walk.'

'Of course you can.'

'Maybe we could walk him together.' Then Philadelphia looked embarrassed at displaying any neediness. She straightened up.

'I've got to go, I have lines to learn

and Roger will tell me off if I don't know them. Thanks for showing me the painting.'

'My pleasure.' Siobhan watched her go.

Fascinating Discovery

As Siobhan got ready to go to the porcelain works, pulling on an old pair of dungarees and a faded T-shirt, she thought of the rumours she'd heard about Philadelphia — that she was vain and silly and liked playing practical jokes on people.

Now Siobhan thought about it, pulling her hair up in a flowered green and pink scarf, she was convinced Philadelphia did this because she liked to be the centre of attention. If she was ignored in her childhood, it was no surprise she craved attention now.

Siobhan herself was lucky to have been adored by her mother, and often told how proud her mother was of her. She was always put centre stage.

She'd been blessed and it made her miss her mother. She sat down and penned a letter to her, pouring out all that had been happening.

Her mother loved to receive a good old-fashioned letter from her daughter and Siobhan realised since she'd been here, she'd neglected her mother in her thoughts. She sealed the envelope and putting on a stamp thought, that's a good job done.

Thinking of letters made her even more eager to get off to the porcelain works and see if there might be any significant letters there which might give her a clue to Marie-Louise's fate. She knocked on Janique's door.

'Janique, are you ready? Louis and I are raring to go.'

Janique appeared.

'Yes, let's go, and I have some home cooked lemonade in the kitchen to take. It gets so hot in there.'

'Home-made,' Siobhan corrected, but the girl's English was coming on well. 'Brilliant, that'll sustain us.'

As they walked down the passage, they bumped into Mariette coming out of her room. She was singing, and looked on top of the world.

'I am going to help Philadelphia learn her lines.'

Siobhan wondered as she watched Mariette skip off down the passage how helpful she'd be but at least Philadelphia had a friend to keep her company and she was pleased for both girls.

★ ★ ★

Janique and Siobhan decided, with Christian's blessing, to take a canoe to float down to the porcelain works on the river.

Louis was happy hunkering down in the centre of the boat. He'd jumped in the water before getting in, to get cool.

There hadn't been rain for weeks, and the river was getting quite low and was safer than it would be in the wetter months. The water was beautifully clear, with shoals of sparkling silver fish darting to and fro in the sunbeams.

Janique manoeuvred the canoe expertly with the benefit of years of experience, as she'd been paddling down here since she was a child. Siobhan sat back, stroking Louis to keep him calm, and looked at the sky, thinking of Marie-Louise's painting.

How many times, she wondered, had Marie-Louise sat in a boat and been rowed down here, perhaps by a lover, maybe someone who lived at La Refuge.

Was it a servant, or the master of the house? Had she been happy or sad and perhaps, in her innocence, been used by someone?

It was so sultry today. Tiny bugs danced in the sunbeams, and the air was like warm treacle. As they passed by the big willow, the water got shallower, there were dips in the riverbed, but also a sort of mound of stones below the water, like a sandbank.

'Zis is so difficult now there is little water,' Janique said. 'I don't know why, but the boat, she is being pulled back to this spot, it must be the current.'

Suddenly, a wave of cold air hit

171

Siobhan. She couldn't understand it. The temperature had shown around 30 degrees on the thermometer in the hallway. Why was it so cold just here?

'I cannot get the canoe away from this spot.' Janique was struggling with the paddle.

Siobhan reached over and grabbed a redundant paddle sitting in the bottom of the boat. She did as Christian had shown her that morning when he'd brought her down here by river. He'd taught her a lot about how to steer a canoe and thankfully, had taught her well.

As the girls struggled, Siobhan couldn't help feeling that forces, curious other-worldly, unknown forces, were pulling them towards this certain spot in the river.

A sense of unease began to creep up from Siobhan's depths and settle in her stomach. What had happened here, she wondered?

She had read somewhere that on occasions, when people visit battle scenes or a house where someone has been murdered, there is a residual memory that remains on the air and seeps into the earth. That where great evil has been done and great tragedy has been experienced, the very soil, the elements, like water and stone retain some of that trauma so that using a sixth sense it can be picked up by people generations later.

Siobhan had that sense now. She shivered. She wanted to get away and back into the warmth of the rest of the river. Preferably, as soon as possible, she wanted to get on to dry land.

'Thank goodness,' Janique said as she finally managed to manoeuvre the canoe away and back off on a current which took them at last to the porcelain works.

'That was curious. I have never known the current to pull like that. We almost got grounded, there is a sort of mound there. If the river gets too much lower, we could have got stuck.'

'Might it be worth asking Christian

to see if he can move it, disperse the mound of stones at the bottom on the riverbed so it is flatter?'

'We have thought of that on occasions when the river is low in summer but Christian fears it might change the flow and cause flooding in winter. He is reluctant to mess about with the route of the river.'

All Siobhan knew as she heard the satisfying plop of their oars in deeper water was that she was pleased they had regained the safer part of the river and were nearly at the porcelain works.

Janique proved herself to be invaluable, particularly in translating the bits of the letters, documents and ledgers Siobhan could not translate herself. Siobhan was pretty good at French and had enjoyed reading French novellas when she'd taken the language at exams in school, although she didn't have the confidence to speak it much.

The two girls had sat for two and a half hours before they made a breakthrough. Most of the documents in the ground floor room were dry and uninteresting. Huge tomes containing lists of orders for multiple porcelain pieces, cups, plates, saucers, ladles and punch bowls, platters and dishes.

Descriptions of the pieces, who had painted them, and their prices were listed with a quill pen in lined columns of neatly flowing copperplate writing.

There were letters from customers ordering more, making enquiries about what could be provided, as well as the odd complaint. These were filed alphabetically together with a painstakingly copied version of the reply that Monsieur Villebonne, the manager of the works, had sent to his customers.

'There's nothing much here of any interest to us,' Siobhan said. 'Apart from the mention multiple times of people's appreciation of Marie-Louise's painting skills and orders asking specifically for items to be painted by her.

'Here's a sweet letter saying how pleased this lady is with the set of vases with paintings of her pet Pekingese dogs executed by Marie-Louise. Let's go upstairs and see what's on the shelves in the attic room.'

They made their way upstairs.

'You start on that shelf, Janique, and I'll have a go at this one.' They'd been there for half an hour before Siobhan turned up something curious.

'Look at this. It's a sort of book within a book.' Sure enough, one of the unwieldy leather bound ledgers had had its inside pages neatly cut out. By doing so, someone had made a sort of hidden box. On the shelf it had appeared like a standard ledger. It was not what it seemed, though, for in the cutaway portion it contained a hidden book. Siobhan took the smaller book out, turning its pages.

'It's a journal!' she exclaimed. 'Oh, my word, someone has gone to great lengths to hide this. I wonder if it will give us a clue to what happened to Marie-Louise.

'This is the room where she worked most, oh, and look — the person who wrote it has illustrated it. There are sketches and drawings.' As she flicked through, more things were revealed.

'Look — here is a sketch of La Refuge. It's pretty good, isn't it, and a sketch of a young girl. Oh, goodness, Janique, I recognise the girl in this drawing.'

'It is Marie-Louise, is it not?' Janique said. 'She looks just like she does in her own self-portraits. Come, let us read the diary.'

It was penned in a simple hand, not quite like a child's but like that of a very young person. Siobhan and Janique poured themselves some lemonade, and gave Louis some water in a bowl they had brought just for him. Then they sat down together and began to read.

'May 1st

My name is Violette Hugo. I am twelve years old today and I write this diary because there are things I am worried about that I cannot tell anyone. My job here at the porcelain works is to do the dusting and the cleaning. I take a dish with water in and sprinkle it on the wooden floors to stop the dust clouding up the air as I work.

Then, I sweep with my big broom and take all the dust downstairs in a sack and out into a big cart to be taken away. All day there is dust from the clay. It makes the ladies who work on the pots, painting and gilding them cough if I do not do my work properly.

I am careful to work very hard and quickly because I need the money I earn to help my poor mama who has six other children. My brother and sisters are all younger than me. My papa died last year of the coughing sickness, so I must take money to Mama each week to feed the babies.

When I visit on Sundays my heart is full when I see the gratitude in Mama's eyes. I do not live with Mama as it is too far for me to walk back to her village each evening so I sleep on a pallet in the attic where the older girls paint.

I like Severigne and Collette, Mimi and Josette. But my favourite painter lady is Marie-Louise. She is very pretty and so kind to me. When the others order me around and make fun of me, Marie-Louise sends me a smile and when the others are not looking, she sneaks me extra bread and even cake if she is given some from the big house.

It is so sweet. Sweeter than the cherries in summer, sweeter than honey from the bees and so is she. But she is sad and that makes me sad, too.'

'May 7th
When I first arrived here, Marie-Louise only thought of her work. She paints the most wonderful things. She is allowed to pick flowers from the garden, and even brought fishes from the river in a glass jar. When she

painted them on the cups they looked real.

'I told her one day that I want to be an artist, to paint on porcelain like she does. So, she has started to teach me. I am not as good as her but she said I can become better, I must just practise.'

Here, Violette had painted some fish and flowers and she had real talent, though it was nowhere near as polished as it needed to be. They read on.

'Every time I try, Marie-Louise says nice things to me and makes comments on how I can be better. Today though, she was different. She would normally concentrate hard on my drawings and talk to me about light and shade and different colours. But today, she kept on getting up from the bench and looking out of the window. It was like she was waiting for something. She was also listening very hard for some sound which did not come. Usually, she talks to me a lot and she likes to hear me chatter but this day she just said maybe we should try to be quiet.

Then there was a sound outside, coming from the river. It was a strange sound. At first I thought it was a bird, but it was not like any bird I know of on the river. It was a sound I recognised because I saw a man in the market on Saturday selling these little things which were like a tiny jug you hold in the palm of your hand.

You put a little water in and you blow and it makes bubbles and whistles at the same time. It makes a noise like a strange warbling bird. This was the sound I heard and as soon as it came, Marie-Louise leapt up and ran downstairs, nearly tripping over her skirts and without even saying where she was going. She just said that she felt hot and needed air.

I jumped on a chair and looked out of the window. I watched her walk swiftly past the men unloading the deliveries from the boat. And I watched her yellow dress disappear along the banks of the river.

Then, by staring long and hard, I saw she was not alone. She met a man, much older than herself and they stood behind the bushes in the trees that they might not be seen though I could see them from high up.

They were together for a long time, talking and holding hands. I saw him stroke her hair. And I saw her look up at him and her face was happy and smiling but then, it looked sad as if knowing him was good but also it was bad. I couldn't see his face at first. But, when they finally broke apart, I saw him go to the big house, and I realised it was the master, Monsieur Gaston.

I was very worried. For I know the master has a wife already. She is a jealous woman with a tongue as sharp as a carving knife. She does not like Marie-Louise. I have heard the other girls say it is because she is pretty and the monsieur is very taken with her.

They said the mistress wanted to send her away but he wouldn't hear of it saying she brought too much money into the porcelain works but now I think there is another reason why he does not want to send Marie-Louise away.'

'May 15th

I saw something today which scared me greatly. The weather is getting much warmer now, spring is giving way to summer and soon we will be scorching up here in our attic. Because I sleep here, I see everything that goes on. I was lying on my pallet asleep when I heard a noise this morning. It was Marie-Louise. She is not usually here this early as she walks from her village to get to the porcelain works.

I pretended I was still asleep when

she arrived, and it was just after dawn. Usually, she is so neat and tidy and proper. But when she came in, her skin was pink with a blush like a ripe peach. It was the same colour as that of my elder cousin when her sweetheart steals a kiss from her when he thinks no-one is looking.

Marie-Louise's hair was a jumble, and the buttons at her neck were open. I watched her as she neatened herself up. Then, when I saw the mud on her shoes, I knew why she was in that state. She had not gone home last night. She had gone somewhere else and stayed there and then had to walk through the dew-soaked grass to get here this morning.

I fear very greatly that she stayed somewhere secretly, in or near the big house. And I do not think she was on her own. For if she was, why would she be so flushed and agitated, why would her colour be so high, as if she was doing something she should not?'

'June 10th

Summer is really coming on now and the days are so hot. We have not had rain for weeks and the river they say is becoming dangerously low. A bad thing has happened. Marie-Louise has become ill, but for some reason she does not want anyone to know. I am so worried about her. It happened like this. I was still on my pallet in the corner, it was first thing in the morning and very quiet before anyone else arrives.

Marie-Louise is the most diligent of the porcelain painters and always first to get here. This morning, she arrived, but before she could even hang up her bonnet, she started retching and making the most awful noises. Then, she grasped for one of the chamber pots and was so sick into it.

I cleared her up with my cloths and water and emptied the chamber pot into the river. I said that I must tell Madam Milon, the lady who oversees all the porcelain painters, but Marie-Louise was terrified at my telling anyone she was ill.

She panicked and clutched me by the arms and made me swear to 'keep all this a secret'. Why should it be a secret? I am so worried.'

'June 23rd

Now I know what is wrong with Marie-Louise and I am even more terrified for her than ever. It happened when she was painting late into the evening. All the other painters had gone home but she was working on a special order she has to finish for a rich gentleman in England.

It is a pair of candlesticks with ivy and jasmine flowers climbing up them. As Marie-Louise was painting, she fell asleep at her bench she was so tired. As she did so, she spilled her water pot all over her skirt, making a blue stain on the grey cotton. I ran to help and told her to take off the skirt so I could wash it straight away in the river.

She was so tired, she let me do it. I had washed out all the stain and was bringing the skirt back to her. I entered the attic room and she was standing in her chemise by the window. As she stood, the last rays of the sun shone on her thin cotton lawn chemise making it transparent. She was rubbing her belly and I saw there was a tiny bulge.

'Oh, heavens,' I said, 'you are with child.'

She sank to her knees and broke down in tears and confessed, and also told me that that night, she was to tell the man who is the father of her tiny unborn baby, of what grows inside her.

For now though, I have run out of space in this diary, this is the last page. I shall begin another very soon.'

And that was it.
'What are we going to do?' Siobhan

closed the diary and held it to her chest. 'What an awful predicament for poor Marie-Louise.'

'We must find the second diary,' Janique said. They searched and searched, dust flying everywhere, the cloying smell of old parchment thick on the air but couldn't find it anywhere amongst the pile of books and ledgers and papers. Nothing.

Even Louis, whose tail was no longer wagging, looked exhausted, hot and panting. He gazed longingly at the stairs as if desperately wanting to go down and out of the stifling attic.

'He needs a walk, poor thing, and I could do with some fresh air myself.'

'And I must help Christian get lunch ready,' Janique said.

The two of them made their way back to the house, both silent, both thinking over what they had learned. When they got back to the house Janique went upstairs to wash her dust covered hands, leaving Siobhan to tell Christian their news.

He, too, looked lost in thought, and so very concerned. His compassion and sympathy knew no bounds. Siobhan realised that this sensitive side of him was drawing her to him like a magnet.

'That poor girl, she must have been in a complete state. What an awful dilemma. And look at you, you are covered in filth. Come with me.' He led Siobhan to a small scullery, a little room she hadn't encountered before but which had a sink, a stool, and was scented deliciously with a bunch of jasmine and honeysuckle Christian had cut from the garden.

'This is the room where I freshen up when I'm gardening. I don't have to take off my muddy shoes because these flagstones are easily cleaned. If you will permit me, Siobhan, you seem to have got a large smudge of grey just here, on your face.'

There was a flannel hanging on a hook which he took off, moistened under the tap, and used to clean first her forehead, then her cheek.

His touch was intimate, and oh so delicious. In the confines of the tiny room, Siobhan was acutely aware of what a large man he was, so broad shouldered, with such strong hands. But they were hands which were also capable of great delicacy of movement.

As he ministered to her, using a little geranium scented soap to rub away the worst of the grime, she couldn't remember the last time she felt cared for in this way. His touch was sensuous, gentle, and the pulse at her neck quickened at the closeness of him.

'Siobhan,' his words were faltering as if he wanted to say something and couldn't. 'I just wanted to say how much . . . how much I appreciate your help in solving the mystery, and how much it means to me to have you here. I wish . . . I wish things were . . . ' She could feel his breath on her cheek now as he looked at her, ' . . . were different. That you weren't still involved with . . . '

'With Gerrard? But . . . '

She wanted to say that she was not

involved, that he was rarely in her thoughts, that it was Christian she thought of last thing at night when she turned out the light, and first thing in the morning when she woke up.

But just as she was about to do so, Janique called from the hallway.

'Siobhan, Siobhan, your friend from Thiviers has turned up, that man, what was his name? Where are you?'

Of all the people to turn up now, Gerrard was like a bad penny. Embarrassed, Christian pushed open the door of the scullery.

'She is here,' he announced to Janique. Then he strode off to his kitchen.

The Wrong Signals

Siobhan grabbed Louis's lead and made her way out of La Refuge.

Gerrard had a swagger about him as he walked down the driveway. It made Siobhan uneasy.

'Hello, Gerrard. I have to take Louis for a walk. Come with me and we can talk.'

That was the only way she could get him alone, to tell him she wasn't interested in them ever getting back together.

She could see Christian looking in her direction as they set off down the driveway and was horrified when Gerrard put his arm heavily and firmly round her shoulder. He was clearly sending everyone signals that there remained something between them.

Christian was too honourable ever to contemplate having a relationship with a woman who was trying to rebuild a relationship with another man, particularly one she'd been engaged to. Gerrard knew that.

He had her shoulder so tightly it was difficult to wriggle out of his hold but by the time she had done so, they had rounded the corner and were out of sight of Christian and the others.

'What do you think you're up to, Gerrard?' She was full of contempt. Louis seemed to feel the same as he growled at Gerrard.

'I don't know what you mean, and what's going on with that dog? It looks vicious to me.'

'Louis is not in the least bit vicious. He's as gentle as a kitten. It's just that he doesn't like to see one person force themselves on another.'

'Don't be silly, Siobhan, you always were apt to turn things into a drama. It must be working with all these actors that does it.

'I just miss our closeness, I miss being together, I miss everything about you.'

The tall poplar trees were waving softly in the breeze, their silver leaves like a thousand medallions on chains. The lane was fresh and green and shady. Wrens hopped in front of them, catching a seed here and a bug there.

Up in the highest tree, one of them sang a tune so melodious and heart-wrenchingly beautiful. Siobhan couldn't help feeling it would have been the perfect romantic scene, if only she wasn't walking here with Gerrard.

Her hand felt empty. She should have been holding the hand of a gorgeous, caring, compassionate, gentle man, like Christian. Instead, because of Gerrard worming his way back into her life, Christian was steering clear of her.

'Gerrard, you might miss me but I don't miss you. I don't know what you think you were doing coming here.'

'You invited me.'

'I didn't!' She was stunned. 'You invited yourself. I was just being polite when I said you could drop in. Why do you twist everything?'

Oh heavens, this was all so difficult. She listened to her own voice which had raised a couple of notches. She knew she was in danger of sounding hysterical and any minute now, Gerrard would accuse her of just that. But, being with someone as unreasonable as Gerrard had that effect on her.

Their relationship had always been exhausting, with highs and lows, like sailing through stormy seas. Louis's ears were back and he was keeping close by her side. She took half a dozen breaths of air, desperate to calm down the anxiety which was churning in her breast like a whirlwind.

You can do this, she told herself. You can conduct a civilised conversation with Gerrard, make your point and tell him to go. You can do it.

The trouble was, he had the knack of making her feel like a petulant child, making her feel guilty for everything. After all, she was the one who had taken the huge step of calling off the wedding.

'I don't twist everything, my darling,' Gerrard said. The endearment made her bristle, she wasn't his darling any more. 'You're overwrought, you've been working very hard and there's all this nonsense about a ghost that you've got wrapped up in. I know you're under stress. What you really need is someone around to support you, to protect you.'

He stopped and turned her to him. He was being gentle now, the way he used to be when he'd been mean and controlling and wanted to win her back. Anyone seeing them together would have thought them deeply in love, any woman would have been envious of her.

On the outside, he looked good, very good. Handsome, in a relaxed and refined way. Public school had taught him to be a charmer.

'The thing is, Siobhan, I love you. I always have and I always will. I can't live without you. Every second away from you is torture. We were made to be together, can't you see that?'

She turned her head from him. She'd heard it so many times before and it was rubbish. It was part of his bid to control her, to own her, and yet, deep inside she felt something melting. Gerrard knew how to press all her buttons. She was afraid of being lonely. That was her Achilles heel and he knew it.

'You're so beautiful, you take my breath away. I was thinking how lovely it would be to go away together. I don't resent you cancelling our wedding, my darling.

'I think it was all getting too much for you, the thought of being the centre of attention. Weddings are stressful, sweetheart, and I mistakenly thought you were enjoying planning our day. I should've been more sensitive, more tuned in to how you were feeling. I blame myself, I'm so sorry. I'll never do that again.

'I was too wrapped up in work and the house and all of those arrange-ments. You can only blame me for loving you too much. For putting you on a pedestal. I remember the first time I kissed you.' He was closer now, dangerously close.

'It was magical, a moment I'll never forget. I'll never have that with anyone else, it's you who makes everything special, Siobhan. I'll die without your love, it was perfect. It can be again. I'll make it up to you.

'You don't have to work all these hours. Let's go away, start again, go on a world cruise. You'll be wined and dined like a princess because you deserve the good things in life. You're special, my darling.'

'Stop, stop!' She backed away, holding her hands over her ears. Louis, sensing tension, stood between them. He was baring his teeth now at Gerrard. She'd heard it all before, torrents of undying love, the sorrys for all the times he'd been pushy and overbearing, the constant refrain that he'd never do it again.

'Why can't you understand, Gerrard?

It's over. The only reason I agreed to you coming here was because I wanted there to be an ending, a full stop we could both live with. I wanted us to part friends and not enemies. But you don't understand because you've never understood.'

She didn't want to be cruel, but she had to tell him the truth.

'You can't love anyone without controlling them totally. You're too much, Gerrard, you're just too much.'

He looked at her, like an eagle might contemplate a frog it is about to drag away in its claws. His eyes narrowed and the corner of his mouth turned up in an almost-smile.

'Your mother doesn't think so.'

Siobhan felt the air rush out of her.

'My mother? What's she got to do with anything?'

'She's really upset, Siobhan, that you called off the wedding. She has fond hopes we're going to get back together. I talked to her yesterday, she was overjoyed about me coming here. It's given her back hope. She wished me luck.'

'How dare you worm your way back into her affections. She has no idea what you're really like.'

He contemplated his expertly manicured nails giving Siobhan a sideways look.

'You haven't spoken to her since you came out here, have you?'

'I can't get a signal on my mobile. I've written to her — I haven't forgotten her.'

'I've had a couple of long calls with her. Told her about the lovely chats you and I have been having. I told her about the cruise, she thinks it's a great idea. She wants us together and for you to have babies, Siobhan, my babies. Why would you deny her grandchildren?'

'That's hideous emotional blackmail, Gerrard. How could you phone and get her on your side without my knowing?'

'It's not just me. Philadelphia's very interested in our relationship, too.'

'What have you been telling her?'

'That we're in love, that we have this sort of tempestuous up and down thing going on. She loves a soap opera, does Philadelphia. She even said it would be a terrible thing if you didn't try to patch up our relationship.

'She went so far as to say she could complain about the way you work if you didn't play ball. She reckons she carries a lot of sway with that director chappie, Roger Rivers. She said there were queues of continuity people after your job.

'She feels sorry for me. She's so wanting to see a perfect love story play out. If I were you, Siobhan, I'd go with it. What have you got to lose?'

My freedom, my independence, my soul. Siobhan was flabbergasted. She'd realised Gerrard was manipulative but she hadn't realised how totally underhand he could be. He really was playing his hand now. This job meant everything to her, but she was in a very precarious profession where the whims of starlets could be pandered to to keep a film in production. No-one would want Philadelphia unhappy.

Siobhan's head started to ache as if there were a thousand tiny hammers thumping on the inside of her skull. She needed to sort this. She needed to speak to her mother. Caroline would be distraught to learn the truth, there'd be a massive meltdown. And yet Siobhan couldn't go back home, not now. That would be death to her career, this was such a big chance for her.

Winning was everything to Gerrard. It didn't matter who he destroyed in the process. Smooth, charming, deadly. Everyone thought he was the greatest catch ever but they never saw this side of him. He kept it carefully hidden. His heart was black. She wished a thousand times over she'd never got mixed up with him.

'There's no way I'm going on any cruise with you, Gerrard. I'm not going anywhere with you.' Louis licked her hand then growled long and low in Gerrard's direction.

'Fine. I'll just have to keep coming round here then. Philadelphia and I get on like a house on fire and she has this girlie thing going of wanting to see you and I reunited. I'll pop around tomorrow and see if you've changed your mind. And the next day and the next.'

'Do what you like. Come on, Louis, we're off.' And with that, she stomped away and left Gerrard standing. He was despicable in every possible way.

A Strange Figure

That night Siobhan had an unsettled sleep thinking of Gerrard's duplicity and scheming. How on earth could she have got mixed up with such a manipulator? But that's how those men worked. They didn't reveal all their cards at the beginning. They started off the epitome of charm and gentlemanliness. They plotted and schemed to keep control of the woman they claimed to love.

It was a strange kind of love that sought to possess at the expense of the individuality of the loved one. She needed a distraction and once she had washed, dressed and breakfasted, she wandered upstairs into the bedroom which housed the mural of Marie-Louise.

Like all the other rooms in La Refuge, it brought her solace. On the wall opposite the mural hung a tapestry. It depicted a rural scene with a town in the distance and in the foreground a goose and a mythical creature with the head of a dog and the body of a bird.

Ringed around the edge was a frieze of acanthus leaves and cherries. The whole was wrought in as many shades of green as the surrounding woodland.

Distractedly, constantly thinking of her conversation yesterday with Gerrard, Siobhan went back to look at the mural of Marie-Louise. There she was, depicted leading the little goat in the pleasant rural scene.

As Siobhan admired the artistry and skill of the leaves on the trees and the swirling waters of the river, she suddenly noticed something extraordinary and unsettling. Hardly believing what she was looking at, she ran out of the room, downstairs and called to Janique who was in the kitchen.

All the others had gone about their daily business. Philadelphia was in the garden with Mariette, supposedly learning her lines. Christian was mending a fence and Roger Rivers was in his room on a conference call.

'Janique, come quickly.'

'What is it?'

'I need to show you something.'

'There,' she said, pointing to the mural, to a spot where the river had been painted in all its azure glory.

'What is eet?'

'It's painted very small, but can you see that figure there? I'm sure it wasn't there when I looked at the mural before.'

'You are right.' Janique peered more closely. 'It is a man, in smart clothes, a man of money. What is he carrying? How do you say it in English?'

As she said the words, Siobhan felt the hackles stand up on her neck and a sick feeling in her stomach.

'We call it a spade, or a shovel.'

'For digging.'

'Yes. For digging. Maybe for hiding a body.' Siobhan feared the worst for poor Marie-Louise.

'That is horrible. How did ze figure get on the mural? The ghost of Marie-Louise must have painted it here for you to see, because you were the one who found the diary yesterday.'

'Seriously, Janique, do you think she's trying to tell us something?'

'Yes.' Janique's eyes were wide with awe. 'The house really is haunted, then.'

'Why, did you not believe it was?'

'I have never really known. People say it is but who can tell? We all see and hear things sometimes I think because we want to. Especially my brother. He has tried for years to solve the mystery.

'It is like 'e wants ghosts from the past to tell him what has happened here. I always felt it was his fancy. Maybe, looking at this, I now believe it, too.'

'If it is Marie-Louise's murderer, if her ghost has painted him in the act of hiding her body, then it means it is down by the river.'

'Look,' Janique said, 'if you look really closely, his other hand, the one zat isn't holding the shovel, it is pointing.'

Siobhan got on her knees, following the line of the pointing finger.

'It's pointing to the centre of the river. Oh my word. That's where we were yesterday. It's where that strange vortex was, the one that was pulling the boat and making it difficult for you to row away. The river will have dropped even more, it was so sunny yesterday and we still haven't had any rain.

'When we were all talking at dinner last night, Philadelphia said she'd been looking at her weather app when she was out in Thiviers yesterday and got a decent WiFi signal. She reckoned the news was going on about drought in this area.'

'What are you two girls up to? I heard my name taken in vain.' It was Philadelphia, who had come in from the garden. Siobhan didn't know why, but she had the feeling Philadelphia may have been outside the room for some time. Listening, perhaps.

She felt sorry once again for Philadelphia. She always seemed to be on the outside of things, as if she didn't fit in with any group. Siobhan would have invited her to help in the search for documents at the porcelain works but she didn't want to make Roger angry by taking Philadelphia away from learning her lines.

'It's scorching out there.' Philadelphia fanned herself with her substantial script. 'Have you found something interesting?'

'Yes.' Siobhan told her about the new figure in the mural.

'Wow, that's cool.'

'We need to get Christian to search that part of the river.'

'Would that be safe?' Philadelphia looked worried. 'You said last night the currents on the river were pulling you this way and that. I like Christian, he's been kind to me and treated me like a normal human being, not fawning round me like men so often do.'

'You're really worried, aren't you?' Siobhan put her arm around Philadelphia wondering why the girl was so concerned. 'Don't worry, we won't let him do anything foolish. We can all go with him and we can make sure he pulls in someone else with a bit of muscle.'

'What about Gerrard?' Philadelphia asked, her eyebrow arching. 'He was telling me he's an expert on boats. Says he goes sailing.'

'I'd rather he didn't come here again.'

'Don't worry if you don't want to ask him. He gave me his number. I'll ask him myself.'

'No please, Philadelphia.' But before Siobhan could stop her, Philadelphia's nails were clicking on her phone. 'There, I've texted him, it'll take him about two seconds to come back to me you see. Hah, I was right, he's up for it. He'll come tomorrow, early. Christian won't be on his own.'

Siobhan was seething. This match-making ploy of Philadelphia's was playing right into Gerrard's hands. The last thing Siobhan wanted was to involve him in anything she was doing. She wanted him to leave her alone.

The only good thing to arise from it was that Siobhan resolved to leave her own important work on the props for that afternoon. She decided to go into Thiviers, find herself a decent phone signal in a café and phone her mother.

Startling Revelations

It was a difficult conversation. There were tears, but Siobhan left her mother under no illusion at all that she was ever going to get back with Gerrard. It was actually cathartic to have a heart to heart with her mother and tell her the real truth about Gerrard's scheming. She'd never really told Caroline because she hadn't wanted to trouble her.

Now, though, to tell the truth had been a good thing, for both of them. Caroline could stop hoping for things that were never going to happen with Gerrard.

'I never want to speak to him again,' she said finally. Caroline's tears had cut Siobhan to the quick. 'Don't worry, Mum,' she added hastily. 'I'm still young. There's still time for me to meet someone really nice and you will have grandchildren one day, I promise you. Just not with Gerrard. That would have been a disaster. It would have tied me to him for life and goodness knows how horribly controlling he would have been with children.'

At least her mother finally knew the truth, and the next day Siobhan woke bright and early.

She was up for searching the river. The water in the river was extremely low now, exposing a large chunk of the river bed. The other thing she was up for was having it out with Gerrard. Whatever the consequences, she must tell Gerrard once and for all they were finished. She felt brave and strong.

As she looked out of the window on to the grounds, she saw Christian getting the boat ready, gathering together tools and rope and shovels. Louis bounded near him and Christian threw a stick for the dog who bounced around him like a puppy. A tide of affection flooded her heart and she realised why she felt so strongly attracted to him.

It was because she knew Christian cared for her even though she hadn't been able to declare to him how she felt.

She knew that his incorrect surmising that Gerrard and she were still lovers was keeping him away. But soon, she would tell him for certain after they'd searched the river, that Gerrard would be off the scene and out of her life forever.

For a second she wondered if she should feel bad about using Gerrard. Then she reasoned that it wasn't she who had invited him to help in the search for Marie-Louise. It was actually Philadelphia. He had wormed his way in, ingratiated himself with Philadelphia in order to manipulate Siobhan, and it was his own fault he was going to have to help Christian dredge the mucky river bed.

Siobhan was able to smile about it. Gerrard hating getting dirty or having his dignity compromised. He got other people to do his dirty work. He employed cleaners and builders and gardeners. He paid people to look after him. By trying to ingratiate himself with Philadelphia, he was going to have to get his hands dirty for once, and Siobhan was looking forward to it.

When Siobhan went downstairs, she found Christian on the phone. She went out on the patio to let him speak in private. But, when he had finished, he came out to find her.

'Siobhan . . . ' He took a seat, letting her pour him a coffee. His lovely face, with its kind eyes was lit with excitement. 'I have more news to add to the mystery we are trying to solve. When you and Janique told me about Violette's diary, I got in touch with a historian I know in Thiviers. I asked him to look up Violette Hugo and see what he could find out about her.

'She is recorded as an apprentice and by all accounts was doing very well. She is mentioned in letters and as a nearby resident coming from a poor but honest family.

'But a strange thing happened. About a year after the date of the diary you found, she was sent away. To Paris, the records say. There is a letter in the local archives, reputedly from an employer there, a portrait painter who had been looking for an assistant. It says she has settled in well and is happy.

'But curiously, thereafter, there is nothing. No record of her even coming back to visit her mother and brothers and sisters. Though there is record of her having boosted the family's finances with a contribution sent each year via her employer until the year she turned twenty-one.'

'Are we to believe then that she forsook her family for the bright lights and the big city?'

'There is another curious thing. At about the time Violette Hugo was spirited away to Paris, her widowed mother was very quickly married to a local man. He was a baker after he married Violette's mother, but what I did not know was that before that, he worked on the boats delivering goods to the porcelain works.

'What's more, Violette's mother was delivered equally quickly of a baby. That baby, a boy called Emmanuel, is a distant relative of mine. The family's fortunes seem to have suddenly blossomed as from being very working class people they seem to have acquired enough money to open a bakery which did very well.'

'Their change in fortune was quite sudden then, and presumably attributable to the money sent from Violette via her employer?'

'True, although my historian friend says that even in Paris, Violette's earnings were unlikely to have been high enough to set her family up in business.'

'That sounds like she was bribed, then, bribed to keep quiet. There is definitely more to this than meets the eye. Do you think it possible that the baby wasn't Violette's but was in fact Marie-Louise's baby?' Siobhan's mind was racing with this new information. That seemed more than plausible.

Gaston, it seemed, had sent poor Marie-Louise's baby away so that his wife wouldn't know of his adultery. Then he had done away with Marie-Louise and made it look as if she had burgled the house and run off.

Not only had he besmirched her reputation and deprived her of motherhood, he might have killed her to stop her telling her secret. No wonder, if that had been the scenario which had played out, she was an unquiet spirit.

'Ah, there is your friend Gerrard. I hope he is up for some serious digging.'

'He's told Philadelphia he is,' Siobhan said. 'Here she comes now.'

Siobhan could hear Philadelphia open the door to Gerrard, giving him the full starlet welcome, complete with air kisses to either cheek as if they'd known each other for years. If Siobhan didn't know better, she'd think Philadelphia was up to something.

Siobhan offered him a cool, 'Hello

Gerrard,' when he came out to the patio. 'Glad to see you've put on your old clothes. But those shoes look a bit smart for dredging the river.'

'I wasn't aware we were going to be dredging, I thought it was just paddling a bit,' Gerrard said, taking a glance at Philadelphia who shot him a huge, innocent smile.

'Do not worry,' Christian said, 'I have a spare pair of fisherman's thigh high boots here, and a spare spade and gloves. Are you ready?'

'Yes . . . ' Gerrard hesitated, 'I suppose so.'

It looked for all the world as if Philadelphia may have been economical with the truth when she'd invited Gerrard to take part. They trooped off down to the river, closely followed by Mariette and Janique. Mariette winked at Philadelphia in an aside that only Siobhan noticed. The two girls seemed to be enjoying a secret joke.

When they got to the river bank, the water had got so low that the area where yesterday, Siobhan and Janique had felt the odd pull in the current was completely drained of water.

In the centre of the river was a mound of stones and mud, and the water was so low that the two men were able to walk out in their waders and reach it easily. Christian had brought round all of the canoes that had been stored in the boat house and these stood bobbing on the low water.

'Right,' he said. 'This is where we start digging.'

It wasn't easy. Soon, the two men were dripping with sweat as they shovelled quantities of stones and mud and threw them in the canoe. Each time they filled a canoe, it was the girls' job to pull it aside and move it to the side of the riverbank so the filled canoes didn't get in the men's way.

Soon, ten canoes had been filled with mud and the mound had been reduced to a hole right in the centre of the river. It resembled a crater where Christian had carefully shored up the stones in a circle so that they could dig the centre out without it filling. The river being so low meant the area was akin to a causeway though it would only stay like that until it next rained. They were all aware this might be the last chance to find out Marie-Louise's whereabouts.

'It's time to get some drinks in — lemonade all round?' Siobhan asked.

'That would be great.' Christian nodded.

'Right, I'm stopping, I'm fed up, we're getting nowhere. I've never believed all this rubbish about a ghost and we don't even know what we're looking for. This is a wild goose chase.' Gerrard was hot and bad tempered. His demeanour of charmer had been eroded and the real Gerrard was being revealed.

'Oh come on, Gerrard,' Philadelphia said. 'If Christian's going to carry on, the least you can do is keep him company. Can't you take the pace? You've got to keep going, at least until we come back with the lemonade.

'I'll give you a hand, Siobhan. We won't be long, and we'll be able to see you from the window and make sure you're not slacking.'

Siobhan was bemused. Philadelphia had never been one to give anyone a hand. What's more, Siobhan had the distinct notion she was playing a game with Gerrard. As she and Philadelphia stood in the kitchen, cracking ice cubes out of their trays, Siobhan turned to her.

'What was the real reason you invited Gerrard here today?'

'You're no fool, are you? There's no pulling the wool over your eyes. It's because,' Philadelphia said with a mischievous smile on her face, 'Gerrard is a pompous bully, and he needed to be taught a lesson.'

'What?' Siobhan was amazed. Had Philadelphia managed to suss out Gerrard's character in such a short space of time? The girl had hidden depths. She might look like a bimbo with an empty head but there was a lot going on inside it, which Siobhan was ashamed to admit she hadn't realised.

'Oh yes, I knew the moment I first encountered that intense come hither smile of his. I've met so many types like him since I've been in modelling and show business.

'Those two professions attract young, innocent, sweet girls who fall for those sort of guys every time. They're rich, charming and they're players.

'They don't so much fall in love with those girls as want to control them. They want to be their masters, having the girls run around after them like lapdogs. There are plenty of girls who simply don't see it coming — they think the guys are in love with them, they believe all that soppy stuff because they're young and sweet and they want to love and be loved.

'Those guys hide their inner selves as surely as a snake hides its fangs. But I've been around a bit, a lot in fact. I could tell Gerrard was trying to get you to go back with him, he told me as much himself. He saw me as one of his armoury of tools. I was worried about you, so I pretended I was interested in him, and your relationship.

'He's so utterly vain and I'm actually quite a good actress. You are going to give him the boot, aren't you, Siobhan?'

Siobhan suddenly felt a rush of affection towards Philadelphia giving her a hug.

'Steady on.' Philadelphia nonetheless looked pleased as Punch at this newfound affection.

'Philadelphia, I'm sorry, I misjudged you.'

'You thought I was an airhead only interested in lounging around swimming pools and drinking gin, did you?'

'Perhaps a bit.'

'Perhaps a lot. And you thought I was flirting with your ex just because I could?'

'Maybe.'

'Perhaps I will get that Oscar one day. I just wanted to make sure you didn't fall under his spell again. He's a great big idiot and you need to keep well away from him.'

'So you wouldn't mind if he never came back again?'

'Yup, that's exactly it.'

'He told me you were dead keen on seeing the two of us reunited and that you might go off in a huff if he didn't stick around.'

'It's exactly the sort of rubbish thing those guys come up with. Believe me, I know. My step-father was very similar. Good looking, a charmer, a wheeler dealer. Everyone else thought he was just a cheeky chappy but he led my poor mum a dog's life. She was just his servant and in fear of incurring his anger twenty-four hours a day.

'Guys like that rely on hooking in decent women like you, who don't want to upset the apple cart, who give in because you want to make everything nice for everyone. That's what bullies like Gerrard rely on. What's more, they frighten off other guys like Christian who really care for you.' Siobhan blushed.

'And I think you care for him, don't you?'

Siobhan didn't need to reply.

'Sweetheart, I've seen the way you two look at each other, it's in your eyes,' Philadelphia continued.' As I see it, Gerrard's the sort of man who looks on the surface like an Alpha hero. He has the money, the clothes, the grooming. He turns on the charm like a tap.

'Christian, on the other hand, appears to be a Beta hero, that's how we class them in the film and fiction world. And yet, really it's Christian who is your Alpha. He's the one I'd want to be with if I was yelling for help from the window of a burning building.

'He's the one who'd rush in without any thought for himself. Whereas Gerrard — well, he'd be worrying his expensive suit might get singed before he'd do anything and even then, it would only be to call for the fire brigade.

'Yes,' Philadelphia added, 'I'd be happy to see Gerrard out of your life. You deserve better. Although I don't think he should go before he's finished digging that dirty great big hole with Christian.

'Gerrard needs to be brought down a peg or two. Did you see him turn his nose up at getting mud on his face? I'll bet the only thing he's ever had on those cheeks is Chanel moisturiser.'

The two girls collapsed into laughter.

'You're a beautiful woman, Siobhan, bright and creative with a super figure and heaps for a man to love. I'm not surprised Christian's buzzing round you.'

Siobhan blushed and realised Philadelphia wasn't half bad after all. She had a good heart, she just hid it well, behind a hard-bitten but very beautiful exterior.

Siobhan's mother had always envisaged her having a knight in shining armour. Caroline had made Siobhan reliant on a man to make her happy but

Siobhan now realised happiness comes from within oneself. A life partner can enhance happiness but she didn't need to look for a pale facsimile like Gerrard. She didn't need second best.

As they took the tray, jugs and glasses outside, Siobhan suddenly felt a weight had lifted off her. She'd been foolish to let Gerrard sneak back into her life. She had allowed him again to call the shots just because she was scared of being alone. Philadelphia had seen right through him, and she'd done her best to help Siobhan realise what was going on.

Dramatic Find

Back at the dig, they all gave themselves a 15-minute break, polishing off the cooling citrus drink, rubbing cubes of ice over their foreheads.

'Is that it for the day then? We haven't found anything. I reckon it's time to pack up.' Gerrard frowned, sweat dripping off his nose, mud splattered across his face.

He really did look ridiculous. Suddenly, Siobhan had the feeling she could see right through him, in the way Philadelphia had been able to. He wasn't exactly a team player, it was all about what he wanted. It always had been.

'It would be a shame to pack up now,' Philadelphia said, batting her eyelashes and hooking her hand round his arm. 'You wouldn't want anyone to think you didn't have any staying power or stamina, would you, Gerrard?

'Or that you'd happily leave your friends in the lurch while you swanned off to go and collapse like some Victorian heroine in a faint.'

Gerrard looked annoyed at this slight to his manliness then crashed his shovel in the ground with renewed vigour. It was a contest, and he didn't want to be outdone. Whereas for Christian, this was a search for the truth and it was clear he'd have worked until midnight if he could get to the bottom of Marie-Louise's disappearance.

Christian had his shirt off, his toned muscles rippling with sweat. His arms and chest were steel-hard. He wasn't having any problem keeping going. Gerrard was huffing and grumbling under his breath about being hungry and wanting to jump in a shower. He was acting like a spoilt child.

The contrast between the two men struck Siobhan so starkly. Christian raised his spade and brought it down yet again. Suddenly, instead of sinking into the mud, they all heard a resounding clang.

'What's that?' Siobhan asked.

'I've struck something, something very solid.' In a frenzy, Christian dug harder and faster. Gerrard, simply leant on his shovel and stared at Christian. Christian manfully moved piles of earth so that what gradually appeared was a box. A long, metal box.

'Oh no,' Siobhan said as they all started to realise what the discovery meant.

'It's a coffin. I've seen metal ones like that in a museum. They were used at one time in England to foil bodysnatchers. They're super secure, and watertight.'

It took both the men to haul the coffin to the river bank. Christian brought his toolbox and with some difficulty, prised the lid off the box. They all stood back, and then, as he slid the lid aside, there was a collective gasp. Inside lay the skeleton of a full grown human. All the clothing had virtually disintegrated over the decades, but in the skeleton's hand was a bright blue turquoise charm.

'That must be Marie-Louise. Isn't it sad that the last thing she clutched in her hand was the necklace Gaston must have given her?'

It was the same necklace as in Marie-Louise's self-portrait. Next to this skeleton was that of a smaller, shorter individual, not a child but not quite an adult. They all stared, uncomprehending. It was Philadelphia who was the first to break the stunned silence.

'Who's that with her? That's too old to have been her baby.'

'It must be poor little Violette,' Siobhan said. 'She must have known too much.'

'Look,' Janique pointed, 'at the bottom of the casket, there is a box. Open it, Christian.'

Christian opened the box. Very carefully, he lifted out a book with greying pages but with still legible handwriting. He flicked to the beginning.

'It is the second half of Violette's diary. That's why you didn't find it in the attic, because it was here all the time. And here is a letter with it.'

He unfolded it reverentially.

'This will be the answer to the mystery. He started to read.

I, Gaston Peydoux, write this letter as a confession. The only other creature who knows of this confession is Father Beart and he, of course, is sworn to the secrecy of the confessional.

He has made me write this so that I can put away my demons. I will meet them again in Hell for that is where I am destined to go when I die. I am distraught and my tears wet this paper for I have committed a great sin.

My first sin was to fall in love with a girl, Marie-Louise Thizy, who was young enough to be my daughter and is not my wife. I wish for all of our sakes I had never seen her but the

233

day I did, my fate was sealed, as was hers.

She was more beautiful than a summer's day, more radiant than a rose. I was struck with such an obsession that would not leave me.

I thought about her every second of every day until I knew I must possess her. And possess her I did, briefly. I loved her and she loved me, in secret, where no-one would see us.

Both of us knew it could only end in tragedy. My wife's father, though old is the patriarch of the family.

It is he who owns this house, La Refuge, and the porcelain works. If I were to dishonour my wife in any way, he would destroy me.

When Marie-Louise announced she was with child I was overjoyed. For my wife and I have never been blessed with children.

My joy though was clouded by knowing I could never acknowledge that child, nor my love for Marie-Louise for to do so would mean I would be cut out of the family I had married into. Everything would be taken from me, my father-in-law would see to that.

The night the baby was born, I made Marie-Louise give him up. I had in secret negotiated with the apprentice Violette's mother, to persuade her to take the baby in.

In return I paid her a handsome sum and also said I would consider sending Violette to Paris to work as a proper apprentice in a porcelain works there.

The woman was greedy and jumped at the chance. I swore her never to tell anyone that I was the father.

If my father-in-law had got to know of the birth, he would secure everything, La Refuge and the porcelain works here in Thiviers on his brother's children and I would have nothing. When I discovered that Violette, the little apprentice, knew of our secret, when I found her diary, I was livid.

I admit that that night I had been drinking, drowning my sorrows in a quantity of Bordeaux wine.

One of my men who worked at the porcelain works came to me as he had discovered Violette's diary, tucked away into the roof space of the attic space at the top of the porcelain works.

I immediately stormed out and went with him to find Violette. All I wanted to do was to scare her enough that she never told our secret.

But she was terrified, she wriggled away, escaped our grasp and ran like the wind to find Marie-Louise who was walking home through the woods to her village.

Marie-Louise, out of the goodness of her heart, sheltered Violette behind her skirts and hid behind a tree but we found her. I grasped her by the hair and suddenly, a red cloud came over me, an anger I could not control.

I was in a mess. My world of fine clothes, prosperity, my whole future as a respected pillar of the community was about to crash around my ears.

Ever since I had met Marie-Louise my life had been in turmoil. I blamed that poor, sweet, innocent young woman for my downfall.

My fists gained a life of their own fuelled by Bordeaux wine in my veins.

I raised my hands to her and in a red frenzy I murdered them both. I still see the blood on my hands now.

If I had been on my own, feeling the crushing guilt and not knowing where to turn, I know I would just have gone straight to the mayor and confessed all.

But I was with my worker. He knew that if he saved me and my reputation he would for ever be in my debt.

He suggested a plan, a way out. He carried the two bodies up into a tree and tied them high in the branches. That way, in plain sight they would be ingeniously hidden.

Then, he took a horse and cart and drove all night to a far away town where he obtained this special heavy casket.

Tonight the river is at its lowest this summer and we are to bury the two girls, in secret.

We will lay them together, with the second half of Violette's diary, and this letter confessing all.

If only that foolish girl had not been driven in her girlish way to write everything down, she and Marie-Louise might still be alive today.

She has hidden the first part of the diary so well I have still not found it. I may spend my life looking for it. It will be my curse.

So, tonight I bid farewell to dear Marie-Louise, the girl I wronged so heinously. My torment will be to live with the overwhelming guilt of what I did in drunken madness.

The only saving grace is hers and

my child little Emmanuel who Violette's mother is passing off as her own. I will secure the woman's secrecy by telling her tomorrow that I have found Violette a place in Paris and packed her off.

I will send Violette's mother a regular allowance pretending it is from her daughter, to keep her sweet, and I will tell her that I will be keeping a close eye upon the baby she is raising as her own.

What is more, my worker who has helped me in all this has a yen to be married and Violette's mother is a widow in need of a husband.

She will take him on for the right price and he wants to give up his strenuous work on the boats here. He was a baker and wants to run his own business. That will buy the silence of both of them.

Violette's mother will look after my boy, of that I am sure, she is not stupid. That baby, little Emmanuel, will be my only heir.

That is God's punishment, knowing that I can never tell the world that the boy I love is mine.

I am ruined. Inside I am a broken, broken man.'

Moments to Treasure

'It is signed Gaston Peydoux,' Christian said, folding the letter and placing it sadly back in the box. It nestled amongst the pile of jewels, the string of pearls, ruby ring and diamond necklace Marie-Louise was meant to have stolen when she had supposedly run away. Gaston had had to hide them in the one place where no-one would ever find them.

'Utterly heartbreaking. No-one came out of that well, did they?' Siobhan said. 'But at least you know the truth now. The mystery is solved.'

'And I can give Marie-Louise and Violette the resting place they deserve in the local church and not here in this awful muddy grave.'

Christian was as good as his word, immediately going off to ring the local police and the local priest to come and make the arrangements.

'And now,' he said, 'I am going to go and phone Pierre Seydoux and let him know of the discovery. I don't think he will be very happy.

'He has never warmed to this house although I don't think he even knew why himself. Perhaps this will explain why he never had a good feeling about it once he knows of his relative's selfish act of treachery. He buried two angels that night.'

And Siobhan was as good as her word, too.

That very afternoon, she told Gerrard in no uncertain terms that she never wanted to see him again and that it didn't matter what he thought about Philadelphia wanting them to get back together because he was wrong.

What's more, she informed him she'd told her mother it was all over and that his hold over her was zero, nada, nothing.

As she stood up to Gerrard, she watched him visibly before her eyes deflate and shrink, like a puffed up peacock who thinks it has everybody's attention but then realises everyone has turned the other way. He left in a huff, his pride ruffled.

Philadelphia, who'd been in the next room and heard most of it knocked on Siobhan's door.

'That wasn't fun.' Siobhan felt like she'd run a marathon and it obviously showed. Philadelphia put an arm round her.

'You did the right thing. You don't need someone like that in your life.'

Siobhan nodded. A clean break was best. Then Philadelphia looked a bit sheepish.

'Siobhan, since we're outing secrets and laying everything on the table, I have a confession to make.'

'What's that?'

'You know the little figure of the man who appeared on the mural, the one pointing to the river?'

'Yes.'

'I'm really sorry but that was me, I

painted him on. I used your water based paints — he'll come off, I haven't defaced the mural for ever.'

Siobhan looked aghast.

'Why?'

'Because I felt a bit left out of all the ghost stuff. I always do feel like the odd one out. It was me and Mariette who cooked it up together.

'She's going to have to tell Christian — which she's not looking forward to — though I shall tell him it was me who talked her into it.

'It was a practical joke and I'm sorry now I misled you.

'It was a complete fluke that that's where the bodies were buried, though I did make a B film not so long ago where a guy buries a body underneath a lake and that's what made me think of it.

'There's another thing. That day you and Christian thought you saw Marie-Louise at the window of La Refuge, from the porcelain works. I've got this long blonde wig and Mariette and I took it in turns to be her. I'm so sorry, it was a rubbish thing to do, both to you and to Marie-Louise's memory.'

'I would have been cross at you leading us astray if it hadn't all come right. Come on, let's have a cocktail by the pool. You did us, and most of all Christian, a good deed.'

'But do you really think there is a ghost?'

'I don't know what to think. I really don't know.

'Christian's convinced but then he's been eating, drinking and breathing this whole story since he was a babe in arms.'

'And what are you going to do about Christian? You really ought to tell him how you feel, and that you've seen Gerrard off once and for all. We need our happy ever after.'

* * *

It wasn't until that evening, when everything had calmed down, the police had gone and the reporters who had shown up as if by magic, sniffing out a grisly story, had filtered away, that Siobhan had a chance to focus on the thing that really mattered to her. Christian. She saw him, at the end of the garden, staring up at La Refuge.

She had put on a light mauve cotton dress, its gently gathered neckline off the shoulder.

The evening air was warm and balmy on her skin. The setting sun in the sky seemed more golden, more peaceful than ever. Christian gave her a half smile when he saw her.

'You look very lovely, I suppose you are going out with your man friend this evening.'

'Gerrard? No, I'm never going out with him again, Christian. He hasn't been of any interest to me for a long time.

'I thought perhaps he was, but we were over long before I came out here, it's just that he didn't think so. It's all finished between us and I've made that perfectly plain now.'

Christian's face lit up. The final beams of evening light settled on his tanned skin, and illuminated the copper lights in his hair. The last little wren of the evening sang at the top of its lungs, filling the gently rising breeze with song.

Christian turned to Siobhan and took her hands in his. As he held her, she felt as if she were floating on air. The scent of the evening primrose flowers rose from the sun-kissed earth.

She knew, as Christian took her face in his hands and gently lifted her lips to meet his that she would remember this moment for ever. Her heart skipped a beat as her head tilted back and Christian's arms encircled her in their embrace.

When they finally parted, Siobhan was breathless. No kiss had ever moved her like that, no man had ever made her feel so alive.

Christian stroked her hair off her forehead. The two of them stood with their own thoughts when these were suddenly interrupted. They looked up to the tiny attic window of the porcelain works which Siobhan and Janique had left open the day before to let the air in.

'Look,' Siobhan said, 'is that a face at the window?'

'Not just one,' Christian whispered in disbelief. 'Two. Two girls wronged, but two girls hopefully at peace.'

It was fanciful but could it possibly be true? Siobhan shielded her eyes, it was so difficult to tell.

The light was fading now, playing tricks with her eyes again. Then, suddenly, out of the window flew a white barn owl and quickly behind her, her nearly grown chick.

As they flew on massive wings, eyes wide, the birds turned towards them and Siobhan realised that she could, at a distance, just about have mistaken those big soulful eyes for those of two faces at the window.

She nuzzled into Christian's arm.

'Do you think there really was a

ghost, Christian? Because I'm not sure.'

He looked down at her.

'I believe there was, and I believe that like that owl, the ghosts have now flown, they can rest knowing that the truth is known and they have been properly laid to rest. Also, I have something to tell you, my sweetest Siobhan.'

'Yes?'

'When I told Pierre Seydoux about the diaries, the letter and our sad discovery of those two poor murdered girls, he said he never wanted to see La Refuge again. It was a stain on his family and he wanted to see justice done.

'He says that when the film comes out there will be a heap of bad publicity if he doesn't make amends in some way. He is going to sign La Refuge over to me in its entirety. He said he didn't want to make money from that tragedy. He acknowledges that if I wanted to pursue it, I have a claim to be the rightful heir as I am related, albeit illegitimately, to Marie-Louise and Gaston Seydoux. Their baby Emmanuel was, after all, my distant relative.

'What's more, he does not even want to touch the jewels Gaston buried with Marie-Louise. He wants me to have them to restore the house and the porcelain works as I see fit.'

'That is wonderful news. You have dedicated so much to this house.'

'There are things I would like to do here,' he said softly, 'and maybe then open the house up for people to see the treasures.

'The porcelain works would make a fabulous museum and we can fill it with Marie-Louise's paintings and pieces of porcelain, we can find them at auctions and track them down if we research diligently.

'I will need someone to help. Might you consider staying on after the film has finished and working on La Refuge?'

Siobhan felt herself sinking into those warm, chocolate-coloured eyes and she had a feeling that this wasn't just an offer of a professional partnership.

'Yes, Christian, of course I'll stay. I can't think of anywhere else I'd rather be.'

He leaned into her.

'Not Rome or New York or Frankfurt then?' he whispered. 'You would give all that international travel to stay here in this dusty old pile with me? I love you, Siobhan. We have a whole future to celebrate.'

With that, they strolled along the river bank and back towards the house.

Its lights glowed inside as bright and warm as the light which shone in Siobhan's heart, like a candle.

We do hope that you have enjoyed reading this large print book.

Did you know that all of our titles are available for purchase?

We publish a wide range of high quality large print books including:
Romances, Mysteries, Classics
General Fiction
Non Fiction and Westerns

Special interest titles available in large print are:
The Little Oxford Dictionary
Music Book, Song Book
Hymn Book, Service Book

Also available from us courtesy of Oxford University Press:
Young Readers' Dictionary
(large print edition)
Young Readers' Thesaurus
(large print edition)

For further information or a free brochure, please contact us at:
Ulverscroft Large Print Books Ltd.,
The Green, Bradgate Road, Anstey,
Leicester, LE7 7FU, England.
Tel: (00 44) **0116 236 4325**
Fax: (00 44) **0116 234 0205**

HER OWN ROBINSON CRUSOE

Susan Jones

Serena Winter normally reports on local events for a travel magazine. Now she's landed her dream job in the Caribbean. On the Atlantic crossing, she's seated next to a grumpy stranger: 'Broderick Loveday, doing nothing and going nowhere,' he tells her. Her job is to report back to 'The Explorer' magazine on drunken monkeys and anything interesting in the islands. The kindness of locals — and someone special — keeps her heart in the Caribbean. But what about when the time comes to leave?

HEART OF ICE

Dawn Knox

Germany, 1938. The escalation of anti-Jewish attacks prompts Kurt's mother to send him to England but when he's boarding the ship, he's mistakenly given a stranger's suitcase. Whilst attempting to return it to its owner, he meets Eleanor but his humble circumstances discourage him from meeting her again. Their paths cross later at RAF Holsmere where Kurt is a pilot and Eleanor a WAAF but is there too much death and destruction to consider taking a chance on love?

ONE GOOD TURN

Sarah Purdue

Fiona will do anything for her best friend, even looking after her troublesome dog, Archie. When Archie pulls yet another stunt, this time raiding a picnic at the park, she and Archie are rescued by handsome Tom and his impeccably trained dog, Dixon. When Tom offers to help with Archie's training, Fiona can't refuse and finds herself falling in love. But Tom has secrets which threaten their relationship. Can Fiona learn to trust again or risk losing her happy ever after?

LEGACY OF FEAR

Susan Udy

In a desperate bid to escape the scandal and persecution that follow the unexpected death of her husband, Alicia Cornell flees to the small Cornish town of Poltreath in search of a safe haven. But it soon becomes clear that someone there recognises her — and is intent on blackmail. Suddenly, all the people she knows become suspects. Can it really be one of them? And if so, which one? Is her secret about to be exposed, just when she believed she was safe?

CHRISTMAS AT THE GINGER CAT CAFE

Zara Thorne

Jilted at the altar, Isla Marchant isn't feeling very festive this Christmas. So when her aunt and uncle invite her to run their café while they're away, she seizes the chance. Short one member of staff, Harry Anderton turns out to be the perfect solution when he pitches up in a campervan. Then Isla discovers that there are certain seasonal traditions she's expected to uphold in the café. With Harry by her side, can she contain her growing feelings and give the people around her the celebrations they deserve?

THE GHOST IN THE WINDOW

Working on a forthcoming movie, Siobhan Frost travels to a beautiful French chateau run by the charismatic Christian Lavelle. Having taken the job to escape her failed engagement, she is shocked when her ex, Gerrard, turns up. And when Philadelphia, the starlet appearing in the film, makes eyes at Gerrard, Siobhan is left in turmoil. One thing is for sure — the chateau has secrets and Christian is determined to solve them with Siobhan's help.